T0164284

First published in Great Britain in 2013 by Comma Press.
www.commapress.co.uk
Copyright © in the name of the individual contributor.
This collection copyright © Comma Press 2013.

'Barmouth' by Lisa Blower © 2013
'We are Watching Something Terrible Happening'
by Lavinia Greenlaw © 2013
'Mrs Fox' by Sarah Hall © 2013
'Prepositions' by Lionel Shriver © 2012 was first published in
Red: The Waterstone's Anthology, edited by Cathy Galvin (Waterstones, 2012)
'Notes from the House Spirits' by Lucy Wood © 2012 was first published
in *Diving Belles* by Lucy Wood (Bloomsbury, 2012).

ISBN-13   978 1905583638

The publisher gratefully acknowledges the assistance of
Literature Northwest and Arts Council England across all its projects.

Set in Bembo 11/13 by David Eckersall.
Printed and bound in England by Berforts Information Press.

THE BBC NATIONAL SHORT STORY AWARD

2013

Contents

Introduction

IN 2005, ON Radio Four's *Open Book,* I asked the
revered short story writer Alice Munro, then in her
seventies, why so much of her writing was
preoccupied with sex and death. Her answer was
succinct, as befitting one of the greatest living
exponents of the short form. 'Why wouldn't it be?'
she chuckled down the line from Canada. 'It's all
that matters.'

In one way or another, sex and death feature
in all five short stories in this collection, which
make up the shortlist for the BBC National Short
Story Award 2013, managed by the BBC in
conjunction with Booktrust. In that same interview,
Munro described how in her work she broke all
the rules for writing short fiction, including the
cardinal sin of providing extraneous detail not
essential to the narrative. 'Why for example,' she
demanded, determined to convince me what a
truly awful writer she was, 'could anyone want to
know about the pattern and colour of the carpet
in a trailer house?' But, it's precisely those descriptive
diversions that make a story authentic – the
essential ingredient to any short story worth its salt

– or indeed worthy of inclusion in a BBC anthology.

The ability of the writers collected here, who also scatter similar 'un-necessary detail', is such that they will catapult you to 9/11 New York, as described by a bitter widow with a surprising sting in her tale; behind the dust sheets of an often abandoned house, among ephemeral companions who'll haunt you long after you leave them; on an annual pilgrimage to a coastal caravan site, through the eyes of a child watching her parents' lives unravel; among the planets and constellations, as they reflect and illuminate the discord and despair of a separating couple; and on an Angela Carter-esque escape of the mythological variety, as an overly-revered wife enacts a miraculous transformation. In each of these original tales we enter a world that is at once familiar and yet surprising, each offering a unique and often startling view of society today.

We were delighted this year to be able to zoom in on the contemporary world and to compile a shortlist that is rich in imagination and diverse in style. All human life is present and, though relationships struggle in these pages as they do in life, there are no obvious themes and no typical vernacular. The stories come from writers who grew up in all corners of the country (and one across the pond), as well as from established writers and those we hope are on their way to being recognised as great, having seen off competition from more than 500 entrants to this year's Award.

The 2013 shortlist is all female, which was not something we sought and a state of affairs we only identified after we had decided on our list, as early copies of the stories came without author credits. This year's crop suggests the short story is a form much suited to the innovative brilliance of women writers. From Charlotte Perkins Gilman – author of the enormously influential *The Yellow Wallpaper* – onwards, many favoured short story writers are women. Foremost among them, the aforementioned Alice Munro and Angela Carter, Katherine Mansfield, Virginia Woolf, Daphne Du Maurier, Margaret Atwood, Lydia Davies, Flannery O'Connor, Lorrie Moore and Jackie Kay. Now we have five new names to add to the list of skilled exponents.

I have been enormously aided as Chair of this year's BBC National Short Story Award by four supremely authoritative fellow judges: Di Speirs, Editor of BBC London Readings Unit – BBC Radio 4 is the world's biggest commissioner of short stories – who has been involved with the Award since its inception; novelist Mohsin Hamid, a Booker shortlist-nominee for *The Reluctant Fundamentalist,* whose sense of humour and enthusiasm contributed enormously to the pleasure of judging; Deborah Moggach, who hails from a whole dynasty of authors (her parents, sister and children are all writers), was BAFTA-nominated for her screen adaptation of *Pride and Prejudice,* and whose own novels include *The Best Exotic Marigold Hotel*; and novelist and short story writer Peter Hobbs, whose debut novel *The Short Day Dying* won a Betty Trask Award and who is currently writer in residence at First Story. He displayed an encyclopaedic knowledge of literary provenance for which we were all grateful.

The success of the charity First Story, which promotes creative story writing in some of the UK's most challenging secondary schools, is evidence of the resilience of the medium. Available as it is now on every sort of screen, in bite-sized chunks at flash fiction events, short story festivals and slams, it is the ideal form in which to appeal to a new generation of readers as well as writers. Perhaps the reason it's so appealing to younger readers is that it's a relatively new form. The term 'short story' wasn't even coined until 1884, making it only a few decades older than that 20th century cultural staple, film.

William Boyd, in a marvellous essay 'A short history of the short story' suggests that its defining feature – namely its length – is the source of its curious appeal. A short story is roughly the length of an anecdote, not as delivered by the pub bore but by a skilled raconteur. Its virtue is its brevity and its magnetic pull. There's no time for the gentle build; the writers chance to display his or her gift is as brief as that of any TV talent show contestant. Most of us yearn for escape from the humdrum, and the short story is the perfect vehicle, like boarding a rocket to another universe and still getting back in time for tea. It makes perfect reading in these days of perpetual movement, whether on a plane, boat, taxi or public transport, which can take as long as the three former all put together! Defined by Edgar Allen Poe as a narrative that 'can be read in one sitting,' short stories can be – and increasingly are – read on the morning commute, in a lunch hour, and before falling asleep.

At the end of William Boyd's essay, he likens Virginia Woolf's famous comment about the deceptive ability of a photograph to enhance and highlight the picture of life to the short story's capacity to enlarge our view of the world. 'This gives us, I think, a clue to the enduring power and appeal of the short story – they are snapshots of the human condition and of human nature and, when they work well, and work on us, we are given the rare chance to see in them more than in real life.'

All five stories in this collection give us that rare opportunity – in less than 8000 words – to see more than what's in front of us; to step briefly from our own world into the lives of others and emerge, wiser, sadder, happier, more thoughtful, illuminated or just simply entertained. With one in six adults still struggling with literacy in the UK, it's to all our benefit that we cherish, celebrate and elevate this vibrant and versatile literary form and ensure that what has been described as the golden age of the short story continues to gather momentum.

Mariella Frostrup

Barmouth

Lisa Blower

LEEK NEW ROAD, STOKE-ON-TRENT

The car was second hand: A Triumph Herald soft-top the colour of my daddy's overalls, the peaks around the backlights so perky, Mummy said it looked as if it were taking off with your woman. Daddy would drive. Saturday clothes, chalk-white trainers, Mummy sitting aside of him in the passenger seat surrounded by food: Barley sugars on the dashboard, sandwiches and flasks at her feet – the only time she was ever thankful for being short. She'd be knackered by the time she buckled herself in – baggy-eyed, short-tempered, hair rush-dyed with a home-snipped fringe – she'd been packing and shopping for weeks, filling up a box on the kitchen floor marked 'holiday'. I'd look down on it and think, when I grow up I won't be nothing like you. We'll eat fish and chips twice a week.

Bunched together on the backseat were Nanny and Grandy Jack, Mum's side, suiting their seventies, no passports; Grandy Jack's chest wheezing like a burglar alarm, three inhalers at the bottom of Nanny's bag. They came with two cases – one full of clothes (bought special), the other full of food (how they'd eat at home) – and their black and white portable telly which we'd cram around to watch the soaps. Nanny would press a fiver in my hand for holiday spends and make a big deal out of it, say – 'I know it's not much but we give you what we can' – and that chocolate would rot my teeth.

Then there was my sister. Four years younger, prettier and carsick, she'd be passed around the car to perch on knees, everyone swapping her over when their legs went dead. That's how she'd spend the journey, the potty between her legs, Nanny ragging her hair. Every year we'd squabble over the caravan's top bunk and every year I'd be told – 'It's Looby's turn'. But it never was. She was even carsick on top bunk.

As for me, I'd been fashioned a bench from a single plank of wood that slotted in behind the front seat, forcing Nanny and Grandy to sit with their knees up, my sister's head to nudge the car ceiling. I'd spend the first half of the journey sitting astride of the handbrake navigating – 'Second left at the roundabout,' I'd instruct, and '33 miles to Shrewsbury' – as if Daddy had never been down this road before. Then I'd have to lie down under the blanket, blue flashing lights streaking through the threads. The car would slow, there'd be an accident up ahead; the road dotted with policemen peering into the cars.

The Amoco

We'd get going and stop five minutes later for petrol.

Why didn't you fill up last night?

We'll have wasted the whole day at this rate, won't we, Jack?

Jen's on the till, isn't she?

Every year, the same questions, and Dad never filled up the night before.

He'd ask, 'Does anyone want any chocolate?' and Mum would glare.

We'd watch Dad chatting with Jen on the till. He'd hold up the queue. Jen would wave. Aunty Jen. Sweet-toothed Jen. Nice as you like then she'd blow up like a chip-pan fire. 'Whatever's she done with her hair?' Nan would say, and Mum would tell us that Jen was going Majorca in a fortnight – all six of them, taking her mother, self-catering, only went Greece back in May – and then she'd stare out of the windscreen, her eyes filled with tears.

Dad would be back with a bagful of chocolate – Bounty, Mars bars, Fry's chocolate cream bought special for Mum. 'Jen's looking well,' he'd say. 'Done something lovely with her hair,' and he'd get *the face*. 'For God's sake,' he'd mutter, pulling out of the forecourt, 'we're going on holiday, aren't we?' and we'd finally get on our way.

WILLIAM HILL'S

We'd have gone less than a mile before we'd pull in at the Bookies. The men would get out. 'Just nipping in for my pills,' and Dad would wink. He always called the Bookies his doctors, like Nan always called the Bingo Aunty Doreen's. 'I shan't see you Thursday, I'm going up Doreen's.' And Mum would roll her eyes and scowl. This time, she swung round in her seat and said to her mother – 'Can you believe this? Now, do you see? *Do you see?*'

But it might pay for the holiday.

Get the girls something nice to wear.

Just think, we could all be going Majorca next year.

We're all off to sunny Spain.

But you never win.

Mug's game.

I'm the bloody mug.

Yeah well, you know what you can do, don't you?

We won't be scrimping forever.

I might not stick around to know.

And as the car door slammed shut, Nan would start to tell us the story about the two little girls – one who had a posh pram and one who had a rusty one whose wheel fell off and rolled into the pond.

Always the same stories, always about other people, never any stories about herself. That would be telling.

LOGGERHEADS

Just past Loggerheads and my sister would be sick on the verge. Mum would be with her, holding her hair up in the air. It was so long by then it was a wonder it didn't rip when she sat down. Mum would be shouting at the car.

It's the way you drive, like it's some race track.

You took that last corner on two wheels.

One sat on our knees, the other on a plank. We'll get stopped one day. The police will have us, and then what? *Then what?* I'm pig sick of making do!

And Dad swivels round in the driving seat and says to me – 'Have I ever told you how I met your mum in Loggerheads?'

He has. A million times.

'She was on the back of another man's motorbike swigging from a bottle of sweet sherry and her hair was as dark as treacle. It was love at first sight,' though he's not looking at my mum when he says it. He's looking down at his Mars bar, his stomach lurching at Jen's fingerprints on the wrapper.

My sister gets back in the car. Mum orders Dad to let some air in. Wind those bloody windows down. Let the girl breathe. We get going. Nan shouts for the windows to go up. It's blowing a chill around the back of her neck. Brrr, she goes, and Brrr just in case. 'We should've packed the electric blanket,' she says.

It's the middle of summer. You'll be sweating cobs.

They've given rain all week.

Only till Thursday. It'll pick up Thursday.

Just in time for us to come home.

That'd be right. Typical of our luck, and Mum would pass around the Barley sugars. Dad would fiddle with the car radio. Fleetwood Mac. *I want to be with you everywhere.* We'd sing. We'd get back on our way. Mum reaching over to put a hand on Dad's thigh. She pats his leg in time to the music. He flinches. She moves her hand away and makes a bony little fist she cannot use.

FORD, JUST OUTSIDE OF SHREWSBURY ON THE A458

We called it dinner – meat-paste sandwiches, salt-your-own crisps, apples and pears and what was left of the chocolate. We'd sit in the lay-by, taking it in turns to wee behind the hedge, me and my sister giggling into our crisp bags as Nan coughed loudly all the while she tinkled. We'd have left the house almost two hours ago. Mum would be looking as if she'd walked there. There'd be dents on her knees from where the cooler box had been.

Nan would be back. 'Is my petticoat showing?' Mum would look. Shake her head, offer her a tissue to wipe her hands. Every year the same picnic, me trying to last out a Bounty till Barmouth, and telling Mum – 'If we stopped for fish and chips you wouldn't have to carry the picnic on your knees.'

Me and my mum: We become our own worst enemies and yet each other's only friend.

OR, MONTFORD BRIDGE OFF THE A5

We should call and see Aunty Bobby. We didn't go last year.

Oh here we go.

She'd love to see the girls.

We'll never get there. You know what she's like.

They are her caravans, love.

And they're in their holiday clothes.

What does that matter?

They'll be covered in dog hairs. Filled up on biscuits. That woman will be there. You know I don't like it in front of the girls.

Why do you have to be like that? If it wasn't for Aunty Bobby and her vans, we'd go nowhere!

Do you hear that mother? Can you hear how he puts us down? That's money folk for you. Married beneath him, he has. As if I need reminding.

And husbands are left all the time nowadays, duck. More than one road to take in this life now. You should learn to drive. Your father will pay for your lessons, won't you Jack?

We don't take the turning to Aunty Bobby's and carry on.

DINAS MAWDDWY

We'd see the road sign and hold our breath.

You should've gone through Bala.

You do this every year.

The car's too old for the hill.

What do you want to prove?

The car can't take it. *I can't take it!*

And Dad would shove the car into first gear, an eight-car tailback chugging behind, Nan cowering into her handbag, her hands covering her ears. 'My ears won't pop. I can smell burn.'

Dad would crunch the car into second. It'd labour. It'd be quicker for us to pick it up, walk with it. He'd put the car back into first. The car behind us would toot, flash its lights, start to pull out.

Lord, give me strength! We're all going to die!

There'd be a funny smell coming from the engine, like the front wheels were coming away. Dad would stare straight ahead, determined, and shift into third gear.

First one to see the sea!

He always did want a bit better. Always did ache to overtake.

TAL-Y-BONT

Three miles outside of Barmouth, or thereabouts, and Looby is sick again. The sick is brown. It makes me feel sick too. We all get out of the car to stretch our legs.

'Look at the colour of that sky,' says Mum, and orders Dad to get the camera. He asks where it is. 'Wherever you put it,' she says.

'Didn't you pack it?' he asks, and Mum closes her eyes.

'I ask you to do nothing but pack the camera, fill up the night before.'

It takes just thirty seconds for it to turn nasty under that pink grapefruit sky. I now know why we never have any holiday snaps.

'Just go!' Mum yells at Dad, and her arms are flailing above her head. 'You don't want to be here. For crying out loud, *I* don't want to be here.'

'This isn't about *Barmouth!*'

Nan ushers us back into the car. Let them argue in peace. Me and Looby crouch under the headlamps and count the dead insects. She takes the right, I take the left, the one with the most dead on their lamp wins.

BARMOUTH

It's 1982, around five o'clock. We're at war with Argentina. My dad hasn't yet been called up. He's waiting. The sparkies are next, he says. They'll need sparkies to rewire the guns, keep the power running through the sockets. Granddad tells him to shut up. He doesn't know what he's talking about. You've no idea what war does to a man. Dad says that's exactly the point. He *wants* to feel like a man.

Nan made a face. Barmouth had changed. The sun had gone grey. The women had put on weight. The yobs already out on the lash: Brains in their groins and dicks on their heads, they were looking to hook-a-fat-duck for the night. Dad winds down the window and shouts – 'Get to war! Get to war!' – and my mum thumps his shoulder and tells him to shut up. She says if he got called up he'd shit himself and bend every rule in the book not to go.

He says, 'You really don't know me at all, do you Kath?'

And my mum nods her head and says, 'You're right. You're right. And I'm far too left.'

We drive along the promenade in silence. No jolly holiday for us.

'It's going downhill,' Nan says.

'It looks the same as last year to me.'

'And the year before that, and the year before that.'

'That's the world though now,' Nan still on her own conversation. 'Ugly in heart and ugly in nature. Never thought I'd see the day when the world stopped wearing its Sunday best.'

My dad agrees. 'A country without self-respect is a land without pride,' and my mum groans into the dashboard.

'I don't know why you even come,' says Mum.

'We don't have to come at all,' says Nan. 'What with your father's chest and my knees; we only come because of the girls.'

I see all the things that hadn't changed and cheer at each one. The black spindle towers of the Railway Bridge, the flags at the top of the Helter Skelter, the neon lights of the Prize Bingo, the Shell Shop where I'd buy gifts for school friends, the Smuggler's Rest where I'd be allowed scampi, adult portion, and cheesecake.

We pull into the car park by the beach. I hope it's for ice cream, a cone of chips, but no. Granddad's legs have gone dead again. Nan has to rub at his shins. Mum sprays Ralgex. We all cough. I turn around, straddle the bench the other way, and start to help. Granddad pushes me away. 'You're too old for that,' he warns.

Mum's face reddens. I see her hands are shaking. 'Do you realise how that sounds?' she shouts. 'Can this family show no-one any affection?'

Dad opens the car door but doesn't actually leave the car. He just sighs. Then he sighs again. When I look at Mum she's crying. That's the fourth time today. There'll be a fifth and sixth time before she goes to bed and then in the morning she'll bustle about the kitchen frying-up as if nothing is wrong with us at all.

GWYN EVANS' CARAVAN SITE, LLANBEDR

Granddad asks for a different inhaler. The one that jump-starts his breath. He says he can't feel his right foot and his chest heaved like a tired racehorse. We pull up at their caravan first. It's as brown as a chocolate bar and has nets up at the window, a vase of plastic flowers in the front bay. Dad carries in their cases. Granddad sits on the step of the caravan, wheezing. Nan steps over him. 'We've only just got here and look at the state of you!' and she says she won't tell him again: 'Because you look after, or you're looked after, and, by heck Jack, if you're being looked after, that's the end of it.'

Granddad couldn't retaliate. He'd no clean breath left. Mum told him to breathe in the sea air. It'll do him good. He does as she says but we all know that nothing could do him much good anymore; fifty years of pot-banks fogging up his lungs.

Nan's in the caravan making tea, making the bed, bleaching the toilet, disinfecting the sinks. She tells Mum they'll be over once they've had a brew and unpacked. 'You can grill that gammon,' she says. 'I'll peel some spuds once I've washed my feet.'

Every year, the same blue bowl, bunions soothed, spuds peeled.

GOLYGFA GLÂN

It means beautiful view, or the view is beautiful. Either way, we can see the sea out of every window. I lie on top bunk and listen to the rain. It hammers down like hailstones on the roof and makes the gas bottles sing. Looby is asleep. The potty is aside of the bed on top of her colouring book. Dad has gone down the site pub for a swifty with Roger from the caravan next door. Roger comes up from Solihull with his wife Charmaine every weekend. He has a signed poster of Margaret Thatcher up at his bedroom window and he sells cars, second hand ones, and car accessories like ice scrapers and hub polish that Charmaine, clad in boob-tube and turban, sells from the caravan hatch. He keeps telling Dad that if he doesn't branch out on his own he'll get left behind – be your own boss, cook your own books, life's going to get a lot more selfish, squire – and as he laughs like a drain down his ear, he offers Dad a good price for the Triumph he doesn't take.

Mum and Charmaine don't get on. They kiss each other hello but they don't mean it. Charmaine goes about in a bikini and raffeta wedge heels with matching handbag. Mum covers up because the sun burns her skin and she has to lie down on her front whilst one of us dots her back with Calamine lotion. Before Dad went to the pub, he said – 'The girls are fine. They know where we are. Ask your mother over if you're that worried. And we are on holiday, love. One drink won't hurt.'

There was a lot of quiet before my mum seethed through gritted teeth that – 'This is never a holiday for me.'

BARMOUTH BEACH

It's 1984. The miners are striking back home. My dad is not a miner but he works at the colliery, tinkering, as my mum calls it, with the wires and fuse boxes that keep the lifts going up and down the shafts. He is not striking. He says we live hand to mouth as it is and if he strikes, what will happen to the men who want to work if the lift stops working? 'I couldn't live with that on my conscience,' he said.

Before we left, four men – thugs as Mum shouted out of the bedroom window – sprayed 'rich scab' on our front wall. Mum told them to bugger off back to work and make the most of what they'd got. 'Nothing lasts forever, sunshine,' she shouted. 'It's going to close whether you like it or not.'

Dad put his arms around her and told her he felt really proud. He came out from behind the curtain and said, 'There's my girl. I knew you were in there somewhere,' and that maybe they shouldn't go when it was rubbing peoples' noses in it, but she pushed him away and told him to take her on bloody holiday or else they were done.

There was a time when she would boast to the miners' wives at coffee mornings – 'Of course, I know Jeff's shoe size by wearing his work boots to the dustbin' – though that now seems like a very long time ago.

We all lie on Barmouth beach hemmed in by windbreaks and woollies and sunbathing on pebbles. My sister's still young enough to call it a den. She's making sand pies. Rhubarb and custard, chicken and ham, the shells she collects in her bucket are the spuds and peas on the side. She has never seen things like everyone else. Her world is a coloured-in place. The sand is the colour of tar. The sun is tepid. The wind slaps us about our cheeks. Granddad snoozes in a deckchair, his breathing rugged and raspy, an old raggedy cowboy paperback going up and down on his belly. Nan is sitting aside of him covered head to toe in blankets doing a Word Search. Brrr, she goes, and Brrr just in case. 'I told you we should have come last week,' she moans. 'Blazing sunshine last week. What did I say? I can hardly hold my pen for frostbite!'

'Yes,' snarls Mum. 'I agree. The weather is all my fault too.' And she looks across at my dad who looks out to sea and says – 'There's got to be somewhere better than this' – and he picks up my sister's spade and starts to dig in the sand like a dog.

THE SMUGGLER'S REST

A year later and we come in August for a change, as if the time of year will make the place different. It is not. A storm was brewing, the porpoise were streaking across the bay, I was in love with Bob Geldof after watching Live Aid and said things like – 'Give me your money, give me your effing dinner money' – sometimes with a penknife, most times just the reputation of having the penknife kept the tuck money rolling in – and my sister was sick in three napkins. She'd been allowed the scampi then had had the peach melba. Granddad went to sit outside for some sea air. The waiter brought us the bill. Mum gasped. 'We don't have enough cash.' She rooted in her handbag then turned to my dad – 'Have you got the cheque book?'

'Why would I bring the cheque book?'

'We haven't brought the cheque book?'

'Well, I didn't bring the cheque book.'

'You didn't think to bring the cheque book?'

'Not when the cheque book is always in your bag, no.' And they still don't look at each other in case the other turns to stone.

After the strikes didn't work and the men lost their jobs, Dad took what he could and went in the office as a lackey. Paper shuffling, my nan calls it. Head of paperclips, sarks my mum. Keeping a roof over our heads, shouts Dad, and calls my mum bone idle. We don't get pocket money anymore and we pay for everything with the cheque book. I'm not allowed school dinners and the Triumph sits across the road on empty. Sometimes, Mum has to take shopping out of her basket and leave it behind. She says we'll go back for it but we never do. Nan pipes up – 'Well, just how short are you?' and my dad goes – 'Three or four inches wouldn't go amiss' – but no-one finds this funny.

Mum says it's embarrassing. 'We're £12 short,' she says. She looks down at Nan's handbag.

'Don't even think about it,' says Nan.

'But you get a free holiday, every year, and it's only £12. We'll pay you back.'

'I know you will, we're pensioners,' and Nan finally fishes out her purse then asks for my purse too. 'I know you haven't spent it,' she says. 'And don't look at me like that. Everyone's got to learn.'

My mum's mouth drops open. 'You're not seriously taking her holiday money?'

Nan folded her arms and told me that like the little girl with the rusty pram and the wonky wheel, if you want something nice you've either got to pay for it or go without.

I got out my fiver. It looked so expensive in my hand. Mum cried and left the restaurant. I watched her go and felt sad. She looked so small, like she'd fit in my nan's handbag, and she'd tried, she'd really tried, but I was sad mainly because I wished I'd had the peach melba. It was so much bigger than the cheesecake. When we came back two years later, without Dad and by taxi, The Smuggler's Rest was a Chinese takeaway.

SWALLOW FALLS

I'm 15 and reading a book, swotting up for my GCSE's. I don't remember the book. I'm mediocre in everything, shine in nothing, not quite a plank short of a toy-box but I'm certainly not up there with my sister whose art is already winning prizes. Mum calls out – 'Oi, bookworm, get yourself off up that hill, get the blood flowing, some fresh air in your lungs!'

I carry on reading. I've been up that hill 14 times. I can draw the view in my mind, tell you what shade of green goes where. They trudge off and leave me with Granddad parked up on a rock with the newspaper. He says – 'How's school?'

I think about the girls who don't speak to me. The one that says I copy her hair. The teacher who tells me I upset people, especially the girl with the Demi-wave and the Russian wedding ring on her engagement finger. He tells me – 'You know she hasn't got a dad, so why are you so mean?' I tell him I'm not mean. My dad left too and they make things up. I ask them – 'What is it that I've done to you?' They say – 'If you don't know then we're not going to tell you' – and I hide in the disabled toilets, punching at the spots that are ruining my face.

Nor do I tell him that I've already done it with Christian Davis because the girl with the Demi-wave is doing it with Robbie Hannan, or that I've had a persistent sickness bug since May and no bleed.

'Fine,' I tell Granddad, 'school's fine,' and carry on reading the book.

Now I wish I'd had a conversation with him, a proper conversation between just me and him. That beautiful place, my stupid indignation, him struggling to get his breath when he'd got so much he wanted to tell me about all that he hadn't done with his life.

SHELL ISLAND

I squint in the sunshine at the dunes. I can't remember why I used to beg to come here – sand in the sandwiches, sand in your eyes – 'How long do we have to stay for?' I moan. Mum says I'm not too old for a clipped ear and gives me a warning. I point out that I'm the only person here *with* parents, that most people my age are in Benidorm, Ibiza, Florida, Cornwall – 'Where the fuck's Barmouth?' the girls snide. 'Sounds like a shit-hole to me.'

I think about all those coral necklaces I used to buy them from the Shell Shop. Those little pebble egg-timers, the dead starfish and pieces of sponge I'd buy as bathroom trinkets. I wonder where they all are now. If anybody actually kept them. Why no-one ever bought me presents back from Disneyland or sent me a postcard from St. Ives. I wonder how they're all getting on at Sixth Form College without me, whether any of them care for what it's like to have a baby and let it go without even knowing whether it was a boy or girl. My nan said that way was for the best.

I look at Mum. She looks back. She used to be pretty, used to keep herself nice, and she's started smoking. 'Give us a fag, love,' she says.

'Get your own fags,' I bark, sparking one from the other to make my point.

She looks away quickly and orders my stepdad to have a word with me.

'Don't start,' he says, and, 'don't spoil everything.'

I sneer and flick him the bird. After the divorce, Mum remarried quickly. Registry office, pub grub, dress from Dorothy Perkins' petite section. We weren't bridesmaids. It wasn't that kind of wedding and we didn't know most of the guests. Nan didn't come either. They still weren't speaking at the time. Mum had to give herself away. I said – 'What about a friend? Don't you have a friend who could do it?' – but after she slapped me across the face, I realised that Mum doesn't have any friends. She finds a man and lives through him instead.

My stepdad is called Trevor. *Trefor.* She met him at the site pub the year after Dad left, but we know that's not true. Trefor was always the one who did the odd-jobs on the caravan. The *handyman. Tasgmon.* He always came when Dad was with Roger or had gone to the Bookies, and we were sent across to Nan's caravan to play cards: Because he'll be drilling. There'll be dust. You'll end up like your granddad, living by inhalers. Helping out a mate, Trefor called it, doing a favour for a friend, but he was pretty quick to move into our house and seemed to come with little else but a teaspoon. There were certainly no tools. If you ever ask him where the rest of his stuff is, he grins and tells you that stuff just pins you down. 'You kiddies are all about the stuff,' he says. 'Think life's all about the spending.' Trefor pays for everything with ten pound notes, but he's never got any change when the ice-cream van comes tinkling its bell round the estate.

I think about my dad back at home in his new flat. Turns out Jen never did feel the same way. He left anyway. Mum said – 'It was an affair in the head.' Dad said that wasn't true. For a minute or two he was really in love. We see him every Saturday and then every Wednesday night. We stop over on bunk beds that he has in his bedroom and he sleeps on the sofa in the front room. When we're not there he sleeps on bottom bunk. His feet hang over the end. The duvet covers him like a facecloth. He can only sleep on his side. He says he doesn't mind. He just pretends that he's sleeping in the bunk beds of Aunty Bobby's caravan – 'And I've always got a good night's sleep up Barmouth,' he says.

He makes sure we have a week in the caravan every year. He says it's important for us to get a break. He comes round the house the night before we go to fill up Trefor's Mini Metro at The Amoco. He leaves two Bounty bars in the glove box and sometimes, a Fry's chocolate cream. If he doesn't do this, Mum and Trefor won't take us.

My sister is up in the dunes sketching with gold crayons. Mum and Trefor are sat in a pair of deckchairs swigging from hipflasks, stroking hands. I go and check on Nan. She's been sat in the passenger seat of Trefor's Mini Metro for over an hour just staring out of the windscreen and clutching onto her handbag as if it were about to be snatched. She warns me everyday – 'The world's rotting. Never trust a man who can't put a penny between his eyes' – and I measure the distance between Trefor's eyes and wonder what they see in Mum.

I knock on the window and ask if she's OK. She looks at me. For a moment she doesn't know me and the grip on her handbag tightens. Then she remembers. She breaks out into a smile. It's goofy, like a little girl awarded her first swimming badge. She calls me by my sister's name. I don't correct her. It's good that she remembers one of us. I ask her if she wants an ice-cream. She fishes in her purse and pushes a fiver through the gap in the window. 'Get your granddad a 99,' she says. 'I love to watch Tony Benn licking raspberry ripple off his chin.'

I don't tell her that Granddad's been dead two years on Tuesday. I don't take the fiver either. I'd put money on it not being hers anyway and that she's been rooting in someone else's handbag again down at Aunty Doreen's. Mum says that death can do funny things to a woman. Sticky fingers, light-fingers, butter-fingers – 'She'll be out the other side come Christmas,' she says, coming towards the car. 'Any longer than that and she's just milking it for effect,' and she feeds my nan a couple of Aspirin and opens a flask of tea.

93 SHARROW LANE

I work behind the bar at the local Bingo Hall, gambling with the old, drinking with the pond-life, and if anyone asks I tell them I'm a nurse or studying to be one, and if they ask any more, I point to an old lady whose mind is back to front and say – 'That's my Aunty Doreen, she'll tell you the rest.'

I live with a boy who likes a drink, likes the ladies, comes back to me when he's skint. I spread holiday brochures on the bed, count out my copper collection labelled 'holiday', and check what's left on my visa. We watch Ceefax on the telly, holiday hotspots and last minute deals. We're making a proper go of it now, going to be a full-on couple and probably move into one of those new flats in the middle of town. 'We could go to Malta,' I say.

'Malta's for dead people,' he says.

'We could stretch to Ibiza,' I say pointing at the screen. 'How much do you have left on your visa?'

He reaches for a can and says – 'Put your bikini on. I want to see you in a bikini.'

I do because I can't stop loving him and I want to be loved by someone like him.

Mum calls me later and tells me the caravan's free. I can have it for a week, first week of August and the forecast is good. 'But for God's sake take your sister,' she instructs. 'I'm up to here with her feminist crap!'

My sister's just finished her A' Levels. She's off to London to study fine art. She's just come back from Paris. One of her teachers paid for her to go. She's come home swooning. *Manon* this and *Manon* that. She says it's like they've met before in another life. Mum says – 'Young girls fall in love and young boys trip into the gutter looking for their keys. They don't always remember where they live. And you used to be carsick in a supermarket trolley.' Looby just smiles. Planes, trains, boats and hovercrafts – she'll go on anything with her sketch pad if it gets her the better view, and she tells Mum – 'Gay or not, I'm still too clever to be a slut' – and they haven't really been civil to one another since.

My boyfriend tells me he doesn't want to go to Barmouth. He doesn't know where it is but it sounds shit and he doesn't want to go with my lezzer of a sister either, and – whilst we're at it – I'm done with you too. This is going nowhere. *You* are going nowhere.

'You're dumping me?' and I collapse on the bed panting, I can't get my breath, and he shrugs and says – 'Perhaps, it depends' – and starts to untie my bikini strings.

By the time we get to Barmouth, my sister's full of cold, my Allegro's overheated, and I'm single with cystitis. It rains all week. It hammers down on the caravan roof. The double bed is full of fleas. Looby lies on top bunk sniffing Vicks VapoRub, making lists, reading books on Elizabeth Frink, Mark Rothko, Bridget Riley, dropping tissues on the floor then sketching them. I sit on the toilet sobbing and rolling fleas between my fingers, breaking their backs one by one.

We go to all the old places – Shell Island, Swallow Falls, the Prize Bingo. Everything's lost its spark. The sky is concrete grey. It's like going back to an old lover and realising they're as soiled as you. We eat Cup a Soups, mash up Bounty bars in black cherry yoghurt and huddle under the parasol to smoke. A caravan window opens across the way. 'I remember you two,' she says. 'Always a smile, always excited to be here, now look at you both,' and she shakes her head and snaps the window shut.

The next night, we take a table in the site pub as far away from the fruit machines as we can get and still Charmaine hunts us out. She totters over in leopard-skin and says – 'Divorce didn't buy you Majorca then?' – and asks if we took a wrong turn at the airport. 'Two teenage girls still coming to this squat?' she says, and she's either drunk or she's bored, we still can't work her out, and she starts to quiz Looby about her purple-rimmed glasses and pink and blonde hair, and then guffaws into her Cinzano – 'Lesbian.'

Looby stands up to correct her. 'Actually, it's Louisa,' she snaps. 'And I'd rather live as *I want* amongst women with not a bean to my name, than be like you, living for man after man, because really Charmaine, you should charge for it,' but by this point, she's looking at me.

We go back to the caravan in silence. I open the door, open a can of lager, offer one to my sister and she says no, come on, we're done here, we're done, and then she adds because she's on a roll – 'You need to sort yourself out now, because you know what you are, don't you?'

I offer her some words that describe me. I don't need to be told who I am. But she knocks me sideways when she says – 'No. That's just trendy vocabulary. You're turning into Mum.'

She asks me to drive her home then. I refuse. I say – 'Let's just have a drink, come on, we'll get steaming drunk and call it a wake, start again' – but she calls a cab, catches the train and heads off to university with the clothes on her back and not a care in the world.

The Prize Bingo

The next morning I sit in my car outside the Prize Bingo. The lights are off. The place looks washed up. The windows misted with bad fortune: there are never any winners in there. I wonder where going home is. I call Mum from the payphone in the amusement arcade. 'I'm going to come home,' I tell her, just about hearing her over the *ching ching kerching* of the slot machines. 'I need somewhere to clear my head.'

She says now's not such a good time. She's taken in a lodger. Stepdad's a prick. Divorces are expensive. It's another rebound thing. 'You'll like Alan,' she says. Got a dry-cleaning business apparently, stops Monday to Thursday night in my old bedroom and when he's not overloading her washer with his work-shirts, he keeps on at her about a double bed. 'That's a thought,' she says. 'He could have mine.'

I put the phone down knowing that Alan doesn't sleep in the back bedroom anymore. He's got his double bed at a cut price rent. I call my dad. He lodges with a farmer now, the one who bought the land from Aunty Bobby before she died. He lives in an old bubble caravan in their backyard that reeks of pigswill and chicken shit. He sounds just as sad on the phone. I tell him that old Mr Evans has stuck a note to the caravan door. That he's offered to tow the caravan off site for scrap but it'll cost. Says he's no place on his site for a caravan that rusty, and before I leave, he tapers ticker tape around the awning, its navy blue letters warning – *Dangerous* – to anyone who thinks it's not static. My dad tuts on the other end of the phone. 'What shall I do?' I ask.

Because gone are the days when I could leave it with him. I was 16 when he got laid off at the colliery. 18 when he had his breakdown and came out of it a crumpled crisp packet of a man, muscles disintegrated into the flat tyres and tired clutch pedals of the dead Triumph he clung onto for dear life and nostalgia and which now sits rusting in Aunty Bobby's backyard, part of the chicken coop and overrun with dead flies. He wears a pair of glum tatty eyes that only light up when he sees my mother, and his hands shake from the drink. He blames twenty years down the coalface but lift-shaft maintenance has still not made it onto the compensation lists. He says things like – 'If you don't put money into it, it'll die' – and – 'There's never any future if you've had your power cut.'

I tell my dad I have nowhere to go. I tell him that I've got lost and surely he understands. 'I'm not making it up Dinas Mawddwy,' I say.

He offers me the left settee bunk of his caravan.

The pips run out before I decide.

In the end I call Nan. She's ninety-two now. Catnaps and stews in her armchair, dredging up the past, only just civil to Mum, sucking on Barley Sugars to while away the day. She says I can have the camp bed. She'll put it up for me behind the settee. I cry when I see it. She says – 'that bed's only temporary so look at it and be determined.' Always so muddled these days and yet so wise.

She gives me a fiver and tells me to go and get us fish and chips. The batter makes her sick and they're old potatoes, gone in the water. 'Nothing's like it used to be,' she complains. I tell her that Barmouth's not like it used to be either, that the caravan's on its last legs. Old Gwyn Evans wants it towed off site. She scolds me for being ungrateful. 'Do you know what I'd give to go to Barmouth right now?' she says.

I don't tell her what I've done to the caravan. How I blame Barmouth for so much. That I'm awaiting the police to charge me with attempted arson. That I'm long past caring whether I serve time or not. That only Charmaine knows that I was trying to go down with it. How I'll never admit to anyone that saves my bacon in court.

'Don't you want to see the world?' I ask my nan.

'But I have my world right here,' she says, and I'll never forget that look on her face: The same as it was when Mum found her in the armchair, drifted off to sleep with just a fiver in her purse.

★

Three months later and Dad had Golygfa Glân towed to the farm. He swapped it for his bubble. Gwyn Evans said retro vans were all the rage and Londoners would pay a fortune for a week in them. But they never did and his wife turned it into a potting shed that greets you as you pull into the site. Not that I know this. I've only seen the pictures on the internet.

★

75 KIELDER SQUARE
The council found us a two-bed flat and we've sold the car for peanuts. My daughter has just turned 8. She thinks sharing her bedroom with Grandma is fun.

Mum's at the door – eighty-one now, keys lost again, chocolate round her mouth, Morrison's carrier bag full of sun lotion – 'What have you been doing?' I shriek. 'Where've you been? I've been worried sick, about to call the police.'

I make her tea. Her hands are frozen and her feet have swelled. 'What have *you* been doing?' Mum asks me. 'Don't you go to work?'

I tell her again. Redundant, last October, both of us let go one after the other and we lost the house, negative equity, awful time with the bailiffs, so humiliating on the front lawn: He's gone to his mother's to think.

'You'll want this fiver then,' she says. 'Your dad will never forgive me otherwise.'

I don't know what she's talking about. I tell her – 'You don't owe me £5 and you don't have any money' – and then because the doctors tell you to do so, I add – 'and Dad's dead Mum, so it doesn't matter.'

Mum looks crestfallen. She thought he was washing up.

'No Mum. He's not washing up.'

She takes four bottles of sun lotion out of the carrier bag and tells me they're for the holiday box. I hand her tea and tell her there is no holiday box; no holiday either.

'I do,' she says, perking up. 'I owe you £5,' and she starts reminiscing.

I let her. You're supposed to. It makes her feel well, like she's back in control and I sit next to her and listen. It's an old favourite. The one about the holiday in Barmouth and how we ate at the Smuggler's Rest and didn't have enough for the bill. She doesn't remember where she's just been or that she and my nan kept up a stony silence for getting on three years after that; how that £12 could've been cited in my parents' divorce proceedings the humiliation was that raw, but she still remembers that she owes me a fiver.

Mum takes out her purse and fumbles through the compartments. I take the purse off her, she's all fingers and thumbs, and I notice that it's more photograph album than purse. I take out the photographs and lay them on the table. We laugh at them together. We're all on Barmouth beach, the sky is inky-black, the sea is raging and we look so alive.

'Those holidays were lovely,' Mum says, 'wouldn't change them for the world.'

I show the pictures to my daughter when she comes in from school. I listen to Mum tell my daughter how lucky she was. Then she returns everything to her purse and removes £5. I look at it shaking in her hand. It means as much to me now as it did back then.

No. It means more.

She gives it to my daughter. Tells her – 'I know it's not much but we give you what we can' – and not to spend it on chocolate, which she will because I won't be able to ask her for it. I'd rather go short. So I drink my tea and watch my daughter cuddle up against her, ask if she'll tell her the story about the two little girls – one who had a posh pram and one who had a rusty one and what happened when the wheel fell off and rolled into the pond.

As Mum talks I look at my sister's painting on the wall. It's called 'Plank', dedicated to me, given to me for my 40th birthday. Aside of it is another painting, 'Barmouth', a grubby looking block of brown and raffeta she's told me to sell. 'It'll get you back on your feet,' she says. 'And it's not as if it's a triumph.' Barmouth is worth over thirty thousand pounds.

My Mother's voice drifts back into earshot. 'So, you see, we all start off in a pram. It's only when we see what the other girls have that we want what they have and that's when things get rusty.'

I realise what I'd like to see more than anything in the world and I head towards the phone to finally make that call.

We are Watching Something Terrible Happening

Lavinia Greenlaw

THE SUMMER THAT Mars stood close to the Earth, I went down to the sea each evening. It was shockingly visible and looked like a storybook version of itself – a red swirl, volatile and ancient. Night after night I lay on the sand like a true believer waiting for something to happen and, while nothing changed or moved, the scale of things was different. Space opened up. I felt small and was glad to.

I'd been on the island for several weeks before my husband was able to visit. I relished the quiet and the simplicity as well as the good fortune of being under clear skies at such a time. I thought I hadn't missed him. The night he arrived, I led him to the beach and hurried ahead calling 'Look! Look!

There it is!' I realised then that I'd missed him greatly.

He took my arm as we skittered down the dunes and allowed me to feel as if I'd arranged the whole thing – the warm night, the soft sea, the red planet. We lay on the sand as couples do who've spent hundreds of nights together – close but unentwined. I made myself say nothing about what we were looking at. I let him decide.

'It looks beautiful,' he said, 'and it looks like a warning.'

We'd been married for two years. The acceleration towards a life together and the settling down were over. What next? We went home and a month later I started my new job at the museum. It bothered him that my days were not easy to explain. In the evenings he always had something to say about the closing of loopholes, the tracking of payments, the new ways drug money was being moved around. His work was of such immediate and obvious importance compared to mine. Even so, I had thought that he was proud of me.

'I deal with this world,' he liked to tell people, 'and my wife deals with the others.'

Then one day he said this instead: 'She could be out there discovering new stars and mapping the universe but she spends her time in a basement with a cupboardful of rocks. I just don't get it, do you?'

When he asked me what I did all day that made me so silent when I came home, this is what I told him. The boxes that come to me contain parts of other worlds. I hold a meteorite in my hands and have the same feeling I had lying on the beach and measuring everything I felt against the distance between two planets. It makes me think about what really matters.

'What do you mean, what really matters?'

'What matters is what lies beyond us.' I knew how hollow it sounded and chose not to understand the way he smiled.

I had to go to France to collect some samples from a recently discovered crater in the Egyptian desert. It had been spotted by someone scanning satellite images for evidence of ancient settlements. What he found was a 5,000-year-old crater that was completely undisturbed. Because of the dry desert air, it was pristine. You could trace the direction from which the meteorite fell in the fanning of the sand.

The scientists got there first. They wrote their names on a piece of paper, put it in a bottle and left. When they came back the bottle was gone.

'So?' my husband said. 'They left their names. It doesn't mean they own what's there.'

The acquisition of meteorite samples is not straightforward. As soon as the scene of an impact has been located, the debris is being collected. The locals arrive first, then the dealers and the scientists, all as businesslike and intent as those who work their way through a battlefield taking boots and wedding rings. Most of the rocks disappear into private collections.

Samples from the Egyptian strike had found their way onto the market and some were being advertised for sale at the annual collector's fair in France. We had no other way of acquiring them and had been in touch with the dealers.

'How much will this cost?' My husband was not interested, he was disapproving.

'We're not buying anything, we're being given it.'

'Why would a dealer give you such valuable specimens?'

'We help them.'

'How?'

'We analyse their samples, provide the verification they need in order to get a good price. In return they give us some.'

'You couldn't point to that place on a map,' he said.

Thousands of chunks of rock fall from space every year, some tiny, most small, and now and then something huge. They can land anywhere. You might pick one up on a walk, put it in your pocket and never know that it didn't make its way there through the slow shift of mud and water, the gradual pressure of stone. It fell.

A bombed-out block of offices or apartments so near to collapse that it seems to hang in the air. Whatever was left inside has been abandoned. Men stand around chatting in the warm twilight. Children watch the slow stream of passing cars.

The further we are from something, the more complete the view, the more simple. From space, the cool blue and green of Earth looks impossible to disturb. If we were beings from another planet looking up at it and naming it for one of our gods, it would be a god of calm or peace. Only Earth's no different to any other planet, a chance construction caught up in the push and pull.

And we're just the same. We think it's all about intimacy, about getting inside one another and identifying all the parts but it's not, is it? You need to go on seeing one another from a distance too – as a complete and simple presence you believe in.

A child stands in a sea of rubble clutching a toy car in her hand. Like others in such pictures she's looking into the distance. She's not averting her gaze. It's as if she's looking for a place beyond this place but cannot see where this place ends. There's no flat surface in sight, no pavement or road, just rubble. But she's not going to play with the car, she's holding onto it. It's not as if she knows what she has in her hand. She just doesn't want to let go.

There are all kinds of locked boxes in locked cupboards in locked rooms. They might contain paper or gold, plutonium or guns, diamonds or ashes – the stuff that fixes our making and unmaking. The box I will open this morning contains part of another world. Of the tens of thousands of meteorites that have landed on Earth, only sixty or so have been from Mars and only five of those have been witnessed. This is a piece of one of them. It came from Morocco via New York. I cannot say what negotiations took place. It was picked up within weeks of impact and so is almost uncontaminated. Planetary matter, a witnessed fall, it's priceless.

The meteorite was seen by nomads in the Moroccan desert. They described a fireball, at first yellow and then green. There were two great booms and the ball appeared to break in half. We have a record of their statements. One remembered saying 'It is a miracle.' Another that 'We are watching something terrible happening.'

One thing smashes into another smashes into another. Whatever collided with Mars sent chunks of rock hurtling into space. Think of a god throwing a stone in the air and that stone rising and falling over hundreds of millions of miles, and its journey taking sixty million years. In the vacuum of space it would neither rise nor fall but would keep travelling until it collided with something else or got caught up, as this one did, in the gravitational pull of another planet. Its charred surface records how it burst into flame when falling at a speed at such odds with the thickness of our atmosphere that it scraped against the air and ignited like a struck match. The nomads were watching the end of something that started to happen millions of years ago, hundreds of millions of miles away. Yes, it was terrible.

The sample we have acquired weighs as much as a couple of bags of sugar. It contains an unusual amount of glass, probably formed in the explosion that propelled it into space. This glass may contain pockets which may contain compounds that are evidence of life. If life is found, it'll be life that is long gone, of a kind I cannot envisage and which occurred in a place I'll never go to. Does this seem pointless? Desperate? It may establish a fact but doing so will raise many more questions.

The image that sticks in my mind is not the girl with the toy or the bandaged child but a man standing up to his waist in ruptured concrete. He's between two white slabs that have cracked and tilted. They're ragged-edged and look a bit like jaws. At first I thought he was being rescued but he's not looking up, he's looking down, back into the hole in which he's standing. He's not trapped. The men who surround him are not trying to help him. One's peering into the hole as well but he's standing back. There's little sense of emergency, only the man looking as if he's about to go down inside that tilting concrete, into what he can't see. His right hand is raised, fingers spread as if he's found something to grasp in order to steady himself. There's nothing there but he's grasping anyway. He doesn't look brave or determined. This is just something he has found himself doing. He's hesitating for a moment and trying to find a hold.

I ring my husband again and ask if his lovers had been strangers.

'No one you know.'

'What were their names?'

'I don't know,' he says and then, 'I can't remember.'

I hold the rock in my hands.

Who's to say which of us is entitled to possess such strange and precious matter? Strangeness is what we're all after. Is it not simply human to grasp what we can and to enter the unknown in the hope of meeting something of ourselves within it?

That night on the beach my husband had tried to reach me.

'I'm here,' he said. 'Here on Earth.'
    I did not respond.

This is life. Here and now on the turning Earth. Here where fire rains down and we still walk out under the sky as if one thing will not lead to another, as if we are not here at all but out there watching it happening from an untouchable distance. As if we will not be drawn in.

Mrs Fox

Sarah Hall

THAT HE LOVES his wife is unquestionable. All day at work he looks forward to seeing her. On the train home, he reads, glancing up at the stations of commuter towns, land-steal under construction, slabs of mineral-looking earth, and pluming clouds. He imagines her robe falling as she steps across the bedroom. Usually he arrives first, while she drives back from her office. He pours a drink and reclines on the sofa. When the front door opens he rouses. He tries to wait, for her to come and find him, and tell him about her day, but he hasn't the patience. She is in the kitchen, taking her coat off, unfastening her shoes. Her form, her essence, a scent of corrupted rose.

–Hello, darling, she says.

The shape of her eyes, almost Persian, though she is English. Her waist and hips in the blue skirt; he watches her move – to the sink, to the table, to the chair where she sits, slowly, with a woman's grace. Under the hollow of her throat, below the collar of her blouse, is a dribble of fine gold, a chain, on which hangs her wedding ring.

–Hello, you.

He bends to kiss her, his hands in his pockets. Such simple pleasure; she is his to kiss.

He, or she, cooks; this is the modern world, both of them are capable, both busy. They eat dinner, sometimes they drink wine. They talk or listen to music; nothing in particular. There are no children yet.

Later, they move upstairs and prepare for bed. He washes his face, urinates. He likes to leave the day on his body. He wears nothing to sleep in; neither does his wife, but she has showered, her hair is damp, darkened to wheat. Her skin is incredibly soft; there is no corrugation on her rump. Her pubic hair is harsh when it dries; it crackles against his palm, contrasts strangely with what's inside. A mystery he wants to solve every night. There are positions they favour, that feel and make them appear unusual to each other. The trick is to remain slightly detached. The trick is to be able to bite, to speak in a voice not your own. Afterwards, she goes to the bathroom, attends to herself, and comes back to bed. His sleep is blissful, dreamless.

Of course, this is not the truth. No man is entirely contented. He has stray erotic thoughts, and irritations. She is slow to pay bills. She is messy in the bathroom; he picks up bundles of wet towels every day. Occasionally, he uses pornography, if he is away for work. He fantasizes about other women, some of whom look like old girlfriends, some like his wife. If a woman at work or on the train arouses him, he wonders about the alternative, a replacement. But in the wake of these moments, he suffers vertiginous fear, imagines losing her, and he understands what she means. It is its absence which defines the importance of a thing.

And what of this wife? She is in part unknowable, as all clever women are. The marrow is adaptable, which is not to say she is guileful, just that she will survive. Only once has she been unfaithful. She is desirable, but to elicit adoration there must be more than sexual qualities. Something in her childhood has made her withheld. She makes no romantic claims, does not require reassurance, and he adores her because of the lack. The one who loves less is always loved more. After she has cleaned herself and joined him in bed, she dreams subterranean dreams, of forests, dark corridors and burrows, roots and earth. In her purse, alongside the makeup and money, is a small purple ball. A useless item, but she keeps it – who can say why? She is called Sophia.

Their house is modern, in a town in the corona of the city. Its colours are arable: brassica, taupe, flax. True angles, long surfaces, invisible, soft-closing drawers. The mortgage is large. They have invested in bricks, in the concept of home. A cleaner comes on Thursdays. There are similar houses nearby, newly built along the edgelands, in the lesser countryside – what was once heath.

One morning he wakes to find his wife vomiting into the toilet. She is kneeling, retching, but nothing is coming up. She is holding the bowl. As she leans forward the notches in her spine rise against the flesh of her back. Her protruding bones, the wide-open mouth, a clicking sound in her gullet: the scene is disconcerting, his wife is almost never ill. He touches her shoulder.

–Are you all right? Can I do anything?

She turns. Her eyes are bright, the brightness of fever. There is a coppery gleam under her skin. She shakes her head. Whatever is rising in her has passed. She closes the lid, flushes, and stands. She leans over the sink and drinks from the tap, not sips, but long sucks of water. She dries her mouth on a towel.

–I'm fine.

She lays a hand, briefly, on his chest, then moves past him into the bedroom. She begins to dress, zips up her skirt, fits her heels into the backs of her shoes.

–I won't have breakfast. I'll get something later. See you tonight.

She kisses him goodbye. Her breath is slightly sour. He hears the front door slam and the car engine start. His wife has a strong constitution. She does not often take to her bed. In the year they met she had some kind of mass removed, through an opened abdomen; she got up and walked the hospital corridors the same day. He goes into the kitchen and cooks an egg. Then he too leaves for work.

Later, he will wonder, and through the day he worries. But that evening, when they return to the house, will herald only good things. She seems well again, radiant even, having signed a new contract at work for the sale of a block of satellite offices. The greenish hue to her skin is gone. Her hair is undone and all about her shoulders. She pulls him forward by his tie.

–Thank you for being so sweet this morning.

They kiss. He feels relief, but over what he's not sure. He untucks her blouse, slips his fingers under the waistband of her skirt. She indicates her willingness. They move upstairs and reduce each other to nakedness. He bends before her. A wide badge of hair, undepilated, spreads at the top of her thighs. The taste reminds him of a river. They take longer than usual. He is strung between immense climactic pleasure and delay. She does not come, but she is ardent; finally he cannot hold back.

They eat late – cereal in bed – spilling milk from the edges of the bowls, like children. They laugh at the small domestic adventure; it's as if they have just met.

Tomorrow is the weekend, when time becomes luxurious. But his wife does not sleep late, as she usually would. When he wakes she is already up, in the bathroom. There is the sound of running water, and under its flow another sound, the low cry of someone expressing injury, a burn, or a cut, a cry like a bird, but wider of throat. Once, twice, he hears it. Is she sick again? He knocks on the door.

—Sophia?

She doesn't answer. She is a private woman; this is her business. Perhaps she is fighting a flu. He goes to the kitchen to make coffee. Soon she joins him. She has bathed and dressed but does not look well. Her face is pinched, dark around the eye sockets, markedly so, as if an overnight gauntening has taken place.

—Oh, poor you, he says. What would you like to do today? We could stay here and take it easy, if you don't feel well.

—Walk, she says. I'd like some air.

He makes toast for her but she takes only a bite or two. He notices that the last chewed mouthful has been put back on her plate, a damp little brown pile. She keeps looking towards the window.

—Would you like to go for a walk now? he asks.

She nods and stands. At the back door she pulls on leather boots, a coat, a yellow scarf, and moves restlessly while he finds his jacket. They walk through the *cul de sac*, ringed by calluna houses, past the children's play area at the end of the road, the concrete pit with conical mounds where children skate. It is still early; no one is around. Intimations of frost under north-facing gables. Behind the morning mist, a faint October sun has begun its industry. They walk through a gateway onto scrubland, then into diminutive trees, young ash, recently planted around the skirt of the older woods. Two miles away, on the other side of the heath, towards the city, bulldozers are levelling the earth, extending the road system.

Sophia walks quickly on the dirt path, perhaps trying to walk away the virus, the malaise, whatever it is that's upsetting her system. The path rises and falls, chicanes permissively. There are ferns and grasses, twigs angling up, leaf-spoils, the brittle memory of wild garlic and summer flowers. Towards the centre, a few older trees have survived; their branches heavy, their bark flaking, trunks starred with orange lichen. Birds dip and dart between bushes. The light breaks through; a gilded light, terrestrial but somehow holy. She moves ahead. They do not speak, but it is not uncompanionable. He allows himself, for a few moments, to be troubled by irrational thoughts – she has a rapid, senseless cancer and will waste, there will be unconscionable pain, he will hold a fatal vigil beside her bed. Outliving her will be dire. Her memory will be like a wound in him. But, as he watches her stride in front, he can see that she is fit and healthy. Her body swings, full of energy. What is it then? An unhappiness? A confliction? He dares not ask.

The woods begin to thicken: oak and beech.

A jay flaps across the thicket, lands on the ground nearby; he admires the primary blue elbow before it flutters off. Sophia turns her head sharply in the direction of its flight. She picks up her pace and begins to walk strangely on the tips of her toes, her knees bent, her heels lifted. Then she leans forward and in a keen, awkward position begins to run. She runs hard. Her feet toss up fragments of turf and flares of leaves. Her hair gleams – the chromic sun renders it livid. She runs, at full tilt, as if pursued.

–Hey, he calls. Hey! Stop! Where are you going!

Fifty yards away, she slows and stops. She crouches on the path as he hurries after her, her body twitching in an effort to remain still. He catches up.

–What was all that about! Darling?

She turns her head and smiles. Something is wrong with her face. The bones have been re-carved. Her lips are thin and her nose is a dark blade. Teeth small and yellow. The lashes of her hazel eyes have thickened and her brows are drawn together, an expression he has never seen, a look that is almost craven. A trick of kiltering light on this English autumn morning. The deep cast of shadows from the canopy. He blinks. She turns to face the forest again. She is leaning forward, putting her hands down, lifting her bottom. She has stepped out of her laced boots and is walking away. Now she is running again, on all fours, lower to earth, sleeker, fleeter. She is running and becoming smaller, running and becoming smaller, running in the light of the reddening sun, the red of her hair and her coat falling, the red of her fur and her body loosening. Running. Holding behind her a sudden, brazen object, white-tipped. Her yellow scarf trails in the briar. All vestiges shed. She stops, within calling distance, were he not struck dumb. She looks over her shoulder. Topaz eyes glinting. Scorched face. Vixen.

October light, no less duplicitous than any season's. Bird calls. Plants shriveling. The moon, palely bent on the horizon, is setting. Everything, swift or slow, continues. He looks at the fox on the path in front of him. Any moment, his wife will walk between the bushes. She will crawl out of the wen of woven ferns. The undergrowth, which must surely have taken her, will yield her. *How amazing,* she'll whisper, pointing up the track. These are his thoughts, standing in the morning sun, staring, and wrestling belief. Insects pass from stalk to stalk. The breeze through the trees is sibilant.

On the path, looking back at him, is a brilliant creature, which does not move, does not flinch or sidle off. No. She turns fully and hoists the tail around beside her like a flaming sceptre. Slim limbs and slender nose. A badge of white from jaw to breast. Her head thrust low and forward, as if she is looking along the earth into the future. His mind's a shock of useless thought, denying, hectoring, until one lone voice proceeds through the chaos.

You saw, you saw, you saw. He says half words, nothing sensible. And now she trots towards him down the path, as a dog would, returning to its master.

Nerve and instinct. Her thousand feral programs. Should she not flee into the borders, kicking away the manmade world? She comes to him, her coy, sporting body held on elegant black-socked legs. A moment ago: Sophia. He stands still. His mind stops exchanging. At his feet, she sits, her tail rearing. Exceptional, winged ears. Eyes like the spectrum of her blended fur. He kneels, and with absolute tenderness, touches the ruff of her neck, which would be soft, were it not for the light tallowing of hairs.

What can be decided in a few moments that will not be questioned for a lifetime? He collects her coat from the nearby bushes. He moves to place it, gently, around her – she does not resist – and, his arms reaching cautiously under, he lifts her. The moderate weight of a mid-sized mammal. The scent of musk, gland, and faintly, faintly, her perfume – a dirty rose.

And still, in the woods and on the apron of grassland, no one is hiking, though soon there will be dogs tugging against leads, old couples, children gadding about. Down the path he walks, holding his fox. Her brightness escapes the coat at both ends; it is like trying to wrap fire. Her warmth against his chest is astonishing – for a wife who always felt the cold, in her hands and feet. She is calm; she does not struggle, and he bears her like a sacrifice, a forest pieta.

Half a mile in secret view. Past the sapling ash trees, through the heath gate, past the concrete pit where one sole girl is turning tricks on her board, practising before the boys come, her gaze held down over the front wheels. There are the houses – new builds, each spanking, chimneyless, their garages closed – and he must walk the gauntlet of suburbia, his heart founding a terrible rhythm at the thought of doors opening, blinds being lifted, exposure. Somewhere nearby a car door slams. She shifts in his arms and his grip tightens. Around the bend; he ignores the distracted neighbour who is moving a bin. Up the pathway to number 34. She is heavier now, deadening his muscles. He moves her to the crux of his left arm, reaches into his trouser pocket for the keys, fumbles, drops them, bends down. She, thinking he is releasing her perhaps, begins to wriggle and scramble towards the ground, but he keeps her held in his aching arm, he lifts the keys from the flagstones, opens the door and enters. He closes the door behind and all the world is shut out.

Suddenly his rescuer's strength goes. His arms give. Sensing it, she jumps, her back claws raking his forearm. She lands sheerly on the carpet. She holds still a second or two, shakes, then goes into the kitchen, directly, no investigation of location, and jumps on to a chair next to the table. As if only now, after her walk and purging of the disease of being human, she is ready for breakfast.

These first hours with his new wife pass, not in wonderment, nor in confusion or fugue, but a kind of acute discerning. She positions herself in the house, wherever she fancies, as she might otherwise have. He follows, making sure she has not vanished, making sure he is conscious. The spectacular evidence remains. He is able to approach. He is able to touch the back of her head, under the slim, almost bearded jaw, even the pads of her paws, which are so sensitive her flesh quivers. Like a curious lover, he studies her form. The remarkable pelt, forged as if in a crucible of ruddy, igneous landscapes. The claws that have left long angry scratches on his arm: crescent-shaped, blond and black. The triangular, white-lined ears, with tall, dark guard hairs. The bend in her hind legs; the full, shapely thighs, similar, in a way, to a woman squatting. He studies sections, details. Her eyes, up close, are the colour of the Edwardian citrine brooch he bought her for her birthday.

He speaks quietly, says things she might want to hear, consolations. *I am sorry. It will be all right.* The day is lost. For much of it she sleeps. She sleeps curled on the floor. Her ribs palpitate. As dusk arrives he tries to eat, but can't. He picks her up and carries her to the bed. She repositions and closes her eyes again. Gently, he lies down next to her. He puts a hand to her side, where she is reddest. The texture of her belly is smooth and delicate, like scar tissue; small nubbed teats under the fur. Her smell is gamey; smoky, sexual.

– Sophia, he whispers, don't worry, though she is not, as far as he can tell, distressed.

He closes his eyes. Sleep, the cure for all catastrophes, will bring relief, perhaps even reversal.

When he wakes there is the faint lunar bloom of streetlight in the bedroom and she is gone. He starts up. He moves through the house, desperately, like a man searching for a bomb. No dream could ever be so convincing. He rushes downstairs, and at the bottom treads in something slightly crusted and yielding. Quickly, he searches on. He calls out her name, feeling ever more its falseness.

She is standing on the kitchen table, an unmistakable silhouette, cut from the wild. She is looking out of the French windows at the garden, the nocturnal world. She is seeing what alien sights? The fresnel lenses of owl's eyes, luminous grassy trails, or bats blurting across the lawn? The grisly aroma of what he has trodden in rises to his nose. He wipes his foot on the carpet. He sits at the table and puts his head in his hands. She watches the garden.

Sunday. Monday. He fields phone calls from his and her places of work. He manages to lie convincingly, asks for personal leave. There is no milk. He drinks black tea. He eats cold soup, a stump of staling bread. He puts down bowls of water on the kitchen floor, but either she does not like the purity or the chlorine. He sits for hours, thinking, silent – every time he speaks he feels the stupidity of words. What has happened? Why? He is not able to unlock anything reasonable in his mind. She is in the house, a bright mass, a beautiful arch being, but he feels increasingly alone. He does not let her out, cruel as it seems, though she pays particular attention to the doors and vents where small drafts of outside air can be felt and smelled – he watches her sniffing the seal, gently clawing the frame. If this does not pass, he thinks, he will take himself to the doctor, or her to the veterinary – one of them will discover the truth, the contraspective madness. But then, how can he?

The sound of a key in the front door lock startles him. He has been lying naked on the bedroom floor while she patrols. It is Esmé, the cleaner. It is Thursday. Nine AM. He pulls on a robe, dashes down the stairs, and catches her just as she is coming into the hallway, dropping her bag on the floor, the door gaping open behind her.

–No, he shouts. No! Go away. You have to go.

He puts a hand on her shoulder and begins to manoeuvre her backwards, towards the door. She gasps in shock at such treatment. Her employer is never home when she cleans – all she knows of him is the money he leaves on the table, the addressed letters she moves from doormat to counter, and it's his wife who speaks to her on the phone. She barely recognizes him, and for a moment mistakes him for an intruder.

—What? What? Take your hands off. I, I'll —

She is alarmed, he can see, at the blockade, at being handled by a dishevelled, undressed man. He gathers his wits, releases her arm.

—Don't clean this week, Esmé. We have a terrible bug. It's very contagious. I don't want to risk you getting it.

He is pale, a little crazed, but does not look ill.

—Sophia has it?

—Yes. She does.

—Does she need anything? I can go to the pharmacy.

—I'm taking care of her. Thank you. Please —

He gestures for her to leave. Routed, Esmé picks up her bag and steps away. He closes the door behind her, moves to the hall window and watches. She glances up at the bedroom, frowns, walks to her little blue car, gets in, and drives away. When he turns round the fox is standing at the top of the stairs.

Later that day, tense with anxiety, he leaves the house and goes to the library. He researches. *Delusional disorder. Folie à deux. Poison effects.* Then: *Transmogrification. Fables.* If he can avail himself of understanding, reason, definition... He returns home with medical texts and a slender yellow volume from the twenties. There is little correlation. He is no thwarted lover. Nor are there other symptoms. Most upsetting is the repetition of one aspect: *an act of will.*

So it continues. He enters a room and at first does not notice that she is up on top of the cabinet, on the windowsill, in the sliding food rack, which he has left open. Her poise so still she is entirely missable, the way all wild things are, until the rustic outline comes into focus. The surprise of seeing her, every time, in proximity; a thing from another realm that he has brought home to belong. She sleeps. She sleeps neatly in a circle, tail tucked under her chin. Not on the bed, where he keeps trying to put her, but on a chair seat, in the corner of the utility room. The house is warm but she makes the most of extra heat wherever she can find it — the sitting place he has just vacated, under the boiler. He cleans away the black, twisted scat that he finds, tries not to be disgusted. *If we were old*, he tells himself, *if I were her carer.* He leaves plates of food on the floor, milk-soaked bread, cooked chicken, inoffensive dishes, which she investigates, tries, but does not finish. Instead she looks up at him, her brows steepling, haughty, unsatisfied. Part of his brain will not translate what she wants: that she must have it raw. Her eyes flicker after birds in the garden. Even trapped behind glass, she calculates. The metrics of the hunt. Hating the humiliation, he brings home a can of dogfood, tips the jellied lump out onto a china dinner plate. She rejects it. He finds her licking her lips and trotting out of the kitchen. On the expensive slate floor is a dark patch of saliva — she has licked something up, a spider perhaps.

He cannot speak to her anymore. She doesn't understand and his voice sounds ridiculous to his own ears, a cacophany. She will not tolerate being in the same room for long. She roams, sniffs at the back door. She wants what's outside, she is becoming restive, growling, but he knows he cannot let her go. What would become of her, and, with her, his hope? He inches around the front door when he leaves and locks it behind, is careful when reentering the house. He phones and tells the cleaning woman her services are no longer needed.

And he knows; in this terrible arrangement, it is he who is not adjusting; he who is failing their relationship. So he decides. He buys uncooked meat from the butcher, offal, and in a moment of bravado, throws it onto the floor in front of her. She nips at a purple lobe, then walks away. Surely she is hungry! *You are a fool,* he tells himself. The next day he goes to a specialty shop and brings home a live bird. A pigeon. Its wings are clipped. He sets it on the floor, where it hops and tries to lift. Within moments she is beside it, crouching, lit with energy. He watches as she recoils and then pounces high, higher than she need, in excitement or prowess, and comes down hard on the helpless flurrying thing. She bites its iridescent neck. She twists its head. She is like machinery; the snapping and clicking of her teeth. The lavender breast is opened, there are riches inside. He turns and leaves, feeling sickened. He is angry and ashamed. That she could ever, even before this, be his pet.

It cannot go on – the proof is everywhere. Musk on the doorframes. Stains on the carpet. Downy feathers. And his unnatural longing, which can never be resolved, nor intimacy converted, even as his mind nudges against the possibility. Whatever godly or congugal test this is, he has certainly failed. He decides. He opens the utility door and leaves it standing wide. He sits outside it with his back against the cold house wall. In the garden is a muddy, mushroomy smell – tawny November. Under the trees, husks and hard fruits are furling and rotting. He waits. The pressure and temperature of the house changes, scents enter, great free gusts of coppice and bonfire and heath, and beyond, the city's miasma. It doesn't take long. Her head and shoulders come through the doorway. She pauses, one front paw lifted and pointing, her jaws parted, the folded tongue lifting up. He stares straight ahead. *Just go. Please.* He tells himself it is not a choice. He does not want her to leave and yet he can no longer stand the lunacy, the impasse, his daily torment. Sophia has gone, he tells himself.

She bolts, a long streak of russet down the lawn, between the plum trees, and up over the fence, the white tip flashing like an afterthought.

He feels nothing. Not relief. Not sorrow. That night he leaves the back door standing open, love's caveat. In the morning there are slugs and silvery trails on the kitchen floor, sodden leaves blown in, and the bin has been knocked over. The following night he shuts the door, though does not lock it. His dreams are anguished, involving machinery and dogs, his own brutality, and blood.

Winter. A little snow, which gives England an older, calmer appearance. She has not come back. He worries about the cold, what might become of her, out there. There are distant nocturnal screams, like a woman being forced – are they hers? He checks the garden for signs, prints in the crisp skin of ice, her waste. The line he tells is one of simple separation. The neighbours do not ask further questions. A letter arrives from her place of work accepting termination of employment. All the while the enormity of what has happened haunts him. The knowledge might send him mad, he thinks. One day he will take off his clothes and lie in the street and beat his head with his fists and laugh as if choking. He will admit to killing her, beg for jail, though her body will never be found.

He returns to work. He is polite and, to new workers in the office, sullen-seeming. Those who know him, those who met his wife, understand something important has been extinguished. He cannot quite reclaim himself. He feels victimhood strongly. Something has been taken from him. Taken, and in the absurdest possibly way. He pities himself, abhors his passivity – could he not have done more? After a while it dawns on him that she doesn't want to come back, that perhaps she did not want what she had. *An act of will.* Her clothes hang in the wardrobe, until, one morning – the mornings are always easier and more decisive – he gathers them up, folds them carefully and places them in bags. He goes through the contents of her purse, which offers no enlightening information, not even her lipstick, a red hue women can rarely wear, or the small purple ball, too gnomic to interpret. But these intimate items he cannot throw away. He places them in a bottom drawer.

Enough, he thinks.

He tries to forget. He tries to masturbate. He thinks of others, of partial, depersonalized images, obscenities; he concentrates, but release will not come. Instead, he weeps.

A week later, close to Christmas, he begins to walk on the heath again. That moulted protean place, which he has for weeks avoided. He walks at first light, when the paths are deserted, and the low red sun glimmers between bare twigs. He is not looking. He is not looking and yet he feels keenly aware of this old, colloquial tract of land, with its debris of nature, hemmed in by roads and houses, lathed away by bulldozers. It is fecund. It is rife with a minority of lifeforms. Black birds in the stark arboretum, larval-looking and half-staged in the uppermost branches. The dead grass rustling. A flash of wing or leg. Sometimes he sits for a while, his collar turned up, his gloveless hands on the fallen trunk, whose sap is hard and radiant. His breath clouds the air. He is here, now. He would give himself, except there is no contract being offered.

He might find comfort in the sinew of winter, when nothing exists but that which is already exposed, and so he does, slowly, and as the Earth tilts back towards the sun, his mind begins to ease. To be comfortable inside one's sadness is not valueless. This too will pass. All things tend towards transience, mutability. It is in such mindful moments, when everything is both held and released, that revelation comes.

She appears on the path in front of him, in the budding early spring. He has been staring down at his feet as they progress, at the shivering stems and petals. All around him, the spermy smell of blossom. *Yes*, the world is saying, *I begin*. He looks up. The vixen is on a grass mound, twenty feet ahead. She is like a comet in the surroundings, her tail, her flame. She has her head lowered, as if in humility, as if in apology for her splendour, the black backs of her ears visible. Oh, her golden greening eyes. Her certainty of colour. How easily she can fell him; and he will always fall.

She faces him. He waits to hear his name, just his name, that he could be made unmad by it. She steps into the low scrub of the forest floor, takes a few high and tidy steps, and he thinks at first the wilderness has finally untamed her, she is afraid, about to run. But she turns, and pauses. Another step. A backward glance. What then, is she piloting? Is he to follow?

The old, leftover stretch of heath, preserved by a tenuous council ruling, by councilors who dine in expensive restaurants with developers, has a crock of boulders and hardwoods at its centre. Moss. Thrift. Columbine. Tides of lesser vasculars. She picks her way in, a route invisible to his eye, but precisely marked, it seems. Rock to stump, she crosses and criss-crosses. She knows he is following; his footfalls are mortifying, though he tries to tread respectfully through this palace of delicate filaments. He keeps his distance. He must convey at all costs that he has no intention to touch her, take her, or otherwise destroy the accord. The roots of old trees rear out of the ground, pulling strings of soil up with them. These are earnest natives; they have survived blight and lightning and urban expansion. They bear the weight of mythical, hollow thrones. Lungs of fungi hang from their branches.

Beneath one trunk there is an opening, a gash between stones and earth. Her den. She makes a circuit of the nearby copse, then sits beside the entrance, laying her flaring tail alongside her. Her belly is pinkish and swollen. She is thinner than he remembered, her legs long and narrow-footed, like a deer's. She cocks her head, as if giving him licence to speak. But no, he must not think this way. Nothing of the past is left, except the shadow on his mind. From her slender jaw she produces a low sound, like a chirp, a strangled bark. She repeats it. He does not know what it means. In their house she was never vocal, except with displeasure. Then, from the dark gape, a sorrel cub emerges, its paws tentative on the den-run, its eyes opaque, blueish, until only recently blind, a charcoal vulpine face. Another follows, nudging the first. And another. There are four. They stumble towards their mother. They fit to her abdomen, scrambling for position, stepping on and over each other. As she feeds them her eyes blink closed, sensually, then she stares at him.

Privvy to this, no man could be ready. Not at home, skulling the delivery within the bloody sheets, nor in the theatre gown, standing behind a screen as the surgeon extracts the child. Human inhibition is gone. What he sees is the core of purpose. His mind is stupefied. They are, they must be, his. He crouches slowly.

She is thirled to the task, but not impatient. Before they are done she nudges the cubs away. They nose against each other. They rock, vulnerably, on their paws, licking the beads of milk. A great inspirational feeling lets loose in him. He has sweeping masculine thoughts. He understands his duty. He swears silent oaths to himself and to her: that he will guard this secret protectorate. That he will forego all else. He will, if it comes to it, lie down in front of the diggers before they level this shrine.

They remain above ground a moment longer. They play in silence, programmed to safe mutism, while she watches. They have her full attention. Their coats are dirty, sandy camouflage, but nothing will be left to chance. She curtails their crèche. One by one, she lifts them by their scruffs towards the hole, sends them back inside, and then, without hesitating, disappears after.

As he leaves he memorizes the way. The den is not as far from the path as he thought, dogs off their leads will detect their secretions, but it is secluded, lost behind a sward of bracken. She knows. His head is full of gold as he walks home. He allows himself the temporary glow of pride, and then relinquishes. He has no role, except as guest. The truth is their survival is beyond his control.

He does not return every day, but once a week makes an early foray into the woods. He approaches respectfully, remains at a distance; a watcher, estranged. He never catches them out but must wait for an appearance. They materialize from the ground, from the undergrowth, an oak stump. If they know him they show no indication. Past a look or two – their eyes eerie and hazelish – they pay him no heed. Their mother has sanctioned his presence, that is all. The exclusion is gently painful, but it is enough to see them, to watch them grow.

They grow rapidly. The dark of their faces shrinks to two smuts either side of their noses. The orange fur begins to smoulder. Their ears become disproportionate. They are quick, ridiculously clumsy, unable to control their energy. He laughs, for the first time in months. Then their play turns savage, tumbling and biting. They learn to focus, peering at small moving quarry; they stalk, chew beetles, snap at airborne insects, while their mother lies in the grass, exhausted by them. She brings fresh carcasses, which they tug at, shaking their heads, twisting off strips of carrion. And still she feeds them her milk, though they are two-thirds her size and he can see the discomfort of her being emptied, of manufacturing and lending nutrients. Sometimes she looks at him, as if waiting for his decision.

He is a man with two lives. He works, he holds conversations with office staff, shops at the supermarket. He turns down dates, but seems contented, and his colleagues wonder if he has, without declaration, moved on. Esmé is reemployed, though she is sad Sophia Garnett has left her husband and suspects injustice against her to be the cause – whatever that may be. But she finds no trace of any other woman in the house, no lace underwear, no lost earring or hairs gathered in the sink. He watches men lifting their children out of car seats and up from toppled bicycles. If anyone were to ask, he would say, *I am not without happiness.*

He walks the heath. He monitors the landscape. He worries about the cubs, the multitude of dangers, even as they grow larger and stronger, and he can see all that they will be. They ambush their mother, who at times seems sallow, having sacrificed her quota of prey, having no mate to help her. They show interest in the rubbish of the woods, bringing back wrappers and foil, even the arm of a plastic doll. There will be dispersal, he knows, but not yet. For now, they are hers, and perhaps his, though peripherally. One day an idea strikes him. He goes to the den site. They are not there, but he doesn't linger. He takes from his pocket the little purple ball Sophia used to keep in her purse. He places it by the entrance. The next time he comes it has vanished. He looks around until he finds it, lying under a thornbush nearby. He picks it up. There are teethmarks in the surface, scratches, signs of play.

What will become of them he does not know. The woods are temporary and the city is rapacious. He has given up looking for meaning. Why is a useless question, an unknowable object. But to suspend thought is impossible. The mind is made perfectly of possibilities. One day, Sophia might walk through the garden, naked, her hair long and tangled, her body gloried by use. She will open the back door, which is never locked, and enter the kitchen and sit at the table. *I dreamt of the forest again*, she will say.

It is a forgivable romance, high conceit – he knows. At night he lies in bed, not at its centre, but closer to the midway point. He thinks of Sophia, whom he loved. He no more expects her to return than he conceived of her departure. But he imagines her stepping across the room, bare, and damp from the shower. And then he thinks of the fox, in her blaze, in her magnificence. It is she who quarters his mind, she whose absence strikes fear into his heart. Her loss would be unendurable. To watch her run into the edgelands, breasting the ferns and scorching the fields, to see her disappear into the void – how could life mean anything without his unbelonging wife?

Prepositions

Lionel Shriver

September 9, 2011

Dear Sarah,

I apologize for the formality of a letter, but I can't trust myself to get this out over a glass of wine, especially while still unsure what I want to say.

Trust that I've treasured your friendship always. On that hiking trip through the Sinai desert when we all met, what brought our two couples together was a shared disinclination to complain. Other tourists whined ceaselessly about the heat and the food, but we four were intrepid. When you broke out in suppurating cold sores from too much sun, despite the injury to your vanity you trooped on as if nothing were the matter. Consequently, I'd hate for this letter itself to seem a complaint – but then, maybe it is a complaint.

Your husband died *in* 9/11. My husband died *on* 9/11. So much has ensued from those prepositions, a single one-letter variation in the alphabet.

Oddly, your story is at least as vivid to me as my own, since I've heard you recount it so many times at dinner parties. It's the story that everyone wants to hear. How the offices of David's investment bank had only recently moved to the 89th floor – a step up in every sense, but if only they'd stayed on the 37th David would probably have survived; that day brambled with *if onlys*. The PA announcement that everyone in the South Tower should return to their desks, which lost seven precious minutes to escape before the second plane hit. Your final conversation with your husband. His report that the only working stairwell was billowing with smoke. His intention to head with several dozen others to the roof. The door to the roof being locked, though you only learned that later. The helicopters that never came.

Yet I've told my story seldom. It doesn't feed local appetites. So allow me, this once. In New York, there are thousands of stories like David's now, but only one of Paul's.

Like you, I recall the most mundane details of that morning. As usual, Paul had to be at Shiso by 10am, to do prep for the midtown lunch rush. But he'd decided to drive, in order to swing by one of my clients after work; a two-year-old Basenji had suddenly started peeing everywhere, and I'd agreed to take the dog in for retraining.

Though Paul made twice as much as a chef as I did as a part-time dog trainer, he always put our work on a par. So he left that morning at about quarter to nine, in time to stop by the pet store on Broadway for more dog treats and kibble. He called me a few minutes later, on his way into the store, because on the car radio he'd heard about the 'accident' at the North Tower. We worried about David, uncertain which tower he worked in, while I hurried to switch on the TV. That was the last time we spoke. I forgot to say 'I love you.' We didn't say that all the time. We didn't want it to get tired.

I tried calling you, Sarah, but of course the line was busy. Then the second plane hit, and that's when the horrible realization bloomed for us all: that the first plane hadn't been an accident, either.

I've reconstructed the rest of the timeline, thanks to the Harrisons, about whose circumstances I now know more than I wish. I've finally lost touch with that couple, though they were almost torturously attentive for a while.

Along with their three kids, Joy and Buddy Harrison had gotten an early start after a long weekend upstate, at a lakeside resort they could only afford with post-Labor Day, off-season rates. The day before, they'd shopped at discount outlets to stock up on sports socks, underwear, and family packs of chicken; with luggage as well, their rattletrap minivan was crammed. Around 9:30, they'd been inching down Riverside Drive, listening to the radio like everyone else. Traffic had been bad, and Buddy would be late for work, the kids late for school; no one had yet entered the universe where there was no work, there was no school. The news was distracting, upsetting, so it took them a few minutes to notice that their engine was on fire.

The Harrisons parked at a cockeyed angle at 79th Street, and at least had the wit to drag their kids out before going after the economy-pack toilet roll. Buddy tried calling for the fire department, but 9-1-1 – the number didn't yet seem eerie – was no longer answering.

Driving down Riverside to work, Paul would have spotted a minivan by the side of the road with flames licking from under the chassis. He was the only motorist to pull over; by then, everyone else was already paranoid and doubtless assumed the van was a car bomb. The Harrisons are fiercely budget-minded, and even my beguiling husband couldn't get them to write off hundreds of dollars' worth of discount products. So Paul helped them drag their booty onto the sidewalk, while the fire got worse. Minding the kids, Joy Harrison sidled over to our Volvo, whose radio was still playing. That's when they announced that the Pentagon had been hit. Joy gasped, Buddy rushed over, and they listened for a moment.

Paul was still in their backseat. He must have been overcome with smoke. And then the minivan erupted.

I'll take their word for it that Buddy and Joy 'streaked' to their van to pull my husband from the flames, but by then Paul was badly burned. They tried calling an ambulance, but 9-1-1 was still jammed. Ironically, they could hear a cavalcade of ambulances wailing down the West Side Highway the whole time, only a hundred feet away, but the emergency vehicles were all headed downtown, not to some lowly car fire on Riverside and W. 79th.

This must have been right around the time you called me, Sarah. You were feeling so helpless, unable to reach David's cell; the satellite networks were overloaded. We both gawked at CNN, frightened personally of course, but frightened also in a larger way that was unfamiliar. During one of our gaping silences, the South Tower emitted a great grey plume on-screen and disappeared into smoke, like a quarter-mile-high magic trick. We inhaled together. We held our breaths together. We screamed together. Sharing that moment cemented our friendship for life. I don't regret that.

Meanwhile, I'm told, Buddy Harrison finally carried Paul to our Volvo to drive their rescuer to St Luke's himself. But by then traffic was hardly moving, and they must have lost a lot more time sitting in it.

The hospital called me at 11:30 a.m. They may have tried to get through earlier, but I'd been on the phone with my mother, who couldn't stop weeping.

'I don't understand,' I said numbly to reception. 'My husband had no reason to go downtown.'

Then a doctor got on the line. This was unusually personable service, but you remember – every doctor, nurse, and paramedic was on call, poised, at every hospital in the city, and there was nothing for them to do. Nothing. At least Paul Eisenberg's peculiar misfortune provided busywork.

'Ms. Eisenberg, I should clarify,' said the internist, and then he delivered the verdict that would cordon me off forever, that would exile me in a small, tinny, unimportant world, a tiny, private, incidental world, while the rest of the country lived in the tumult of history, of shifting tectonic allegiances, of wars and counterinsurgencies; of great moral choices, grand speeches, and noble sacrifices: 'as far as we can tell, your husband's death had nothing to do with the World Trade Center.'

In New York City, 148 people die every day – from strokes, traffic accidents, overdoses, or misguided acts of altruism. Ten years ago, my husband was one of them. But because he merely died *on* 9/11, I've been banished from the commemorations to which you've been invited for ten years.

Paul didn't burn himself in Shiso's kitchen, so I've received no survivor's benefits from Worker's Comp. While still childless, Paul and I had seen no reason to carry life insurance. Without a second income, I've had to give up the Upper West Side apartment. I sold most of our furniture. I'm stuck in a walk-up in Queens. Where the supermarket signs are all in Chinese. I can't even afford cable.

So you can imagine it was difficult for me when that Victims Compensation Fund awarded you *2.2 million dollars*. Lump sum, tax free. And you still objected it wasn't enough. It didn't reflect David's lifetime earning power. But Sarah, I lost my husband too. Yet no one's given me a dime, and I still pay taxes on every minimum-wage dog-walking check. That's right, I've been reduced to dog-*walking*.

Everyone who died *in* 9/11 is described as 'a hero.' If you don't mind, David did nothing but go to work. On his own initiative, Paul was helping a family in distress. Paul was a hero. David was a casualty. Yet David's picture was in the paper, not my husband's. David's passing is mourned annually by millions of people, but no one besides immediate family remembers Paul's.

You've always emphasized how losing David was especially terrible because you have kids. Doesn't that make you lucky? You've preserved your husband's very DNA. I have nothing to show for Paul. Some days I can't even remember what he looked like, while your children's faces remind you daily of David's. Remember, Paul and I had just started to try – and I cried myself sick near the end of that September when I got my period after all.

You've been envious that I had a body to bury. Well, don't be. I may have taken possession of an incinerated corpse, but that body has never kissed me goodnight, or promised to pick up kibble on the way to work. It hasn't proved good for much.

You've sometimes strained to include me. True, were the first responders not all streaming downtown – where they would line up, bumper-to-bumper, pointlessly empty – maybe Paul could have gotten to the hospital in time to save his life. Maybe if the Pentagon hadn't just been attacked, the Harrisons would have been more attentive, and dragged my husband to safety. Still, I'm not officially a '9/11 widow', and I've never claimed to be.

In some ways, that cataclysm has been the making of you. Before, you didn't even have a job, and now you give speeches at fund-raising lunches. You delivered a statement to the 9/11 Commission. You get letters published in the *New York Times*, which gives you special credence because of your bona fides. You attend the commemoration every year in smart black suits. You seem to know who you are now, while your children wear their heritage with pride: their father died *in 9/11*.

You have fierce, political opinions, where before they were hazy – which has sometimes put us at loggerheads. I pointed out that the Park51 mosque is planned *near* Ground Zero, not *at* Ground Zero – and I of all people should understand the importance of prepositions. You were offended. The mosque was 'insensitive', you said. But we can't ban a particular religion from a whole area of New York, I said, it's unconstitutional. You just kept repeating that word, *insensitive*. I got the message. My opinion didn't count. Your opinion was privileged.

Sarah, maybe that's what I am trying to say: I know it doesn't seem that way, but you *are* privileged. Around the world, over 150,000 people die every day – from cholera, dysentery, cancer, starvation, war, or sheer neglect. Almost none of their families enjoy the widespread sympathy of total strangers that yours does. David's death means something – not only to you and your kids, but to the city, the country, the world – while all I can construe from the debacle on Riverside Drive was that my husband was a nice guy. The rest of us suffer our losses as deeply as you do, but can make nothing of them. We're left with no large, dark force like 'Islamic terrorism' to locate at their heart, just an ongoing void and inexplicable awfulness. We anguish alone and in silence. Our anniversaries are quiet, dolorous affairs, and the company with whom we share them dwindles.

In primary school, a *preposition* was 'anything an airplane can do to a cloud.' Since flying objects can apparently go *through* and even *out* the other side of tall buildings, perhaps a preposition is now 'anything an airplane can do to the World Trade Center.' Whatever their definition, prepositions are powerful words. *At* Ground Zero, *near* Ground Zero. *In* 9/11, *on* 9/11. Our diverging fates have hinged on one letter. This year, perhaps you can finally afford some backhanded gratitude for that small 'i'.

Your life was shattered on an iconic shorthand, '9/11'; mine fell apart on plain old September 11th, 2001. Your loss has filled you, made you greater, connected you to your neighbors and your country, and raised you to a select elite. My loss has diminished me, as losses diminish most people. I will still join you in spirit downtown this September, and I, too, will sorrow that night as twin spotlights shoot, bend, and evanesce into the sky. But spare a thought for us exiles – the bereaved for no grand reason. Your lot has been hard. But I believe my lot has been even harder. For a decade, the conceit of our friendship has been quite the reverse.

Still with great affection,
Rachel

Notes from the House Spirits

Lucy Wood

THERE IS A sudden silence and then everything is the same. An empty house is never silent for long and a house is never empty because we are here. There is a sudden silence and then everything is the same. Nothing is ever exactly the same, but it goes back to how it was. The staircase creaks and relaxes, the air slows and stills in rooms.

The buddleia in the attic is growing. We dream, as we have always dreamt, of doors and windows under water, of walls under water. We try not to dwell on these dreams.

Dust drifts across the room and settles on skirting and curtain rails. We can see it, every single piece, as it piles up and no one brushes it away. Dust is static and lazy; it lands on the first thing it sees. It fills the house bit by bit and no one brushes it away. It is not our job to brush it away.

★

This one left suddenly in the night. She sat up quickly in bed, swung her legs on to the floor and walked down the stairs. She stretched out her arms but there was no one else there. She talked to someone that we couldn't see. 'There you are,' she said. 'You didn't take your boots off. Will I need a coat?' She went out the front door and she left it open.

Things we glimpse out of the front door:
> Other rooms.
> Other houses.
> One huge space like a silent kitchen, with small lights on and one crescent of light, as if someone had left the fridge door open.

It is rude to leave suddenly, without any notice. She didn't give us any notice. There weren't any boxes. She didn't take any of her things away. Didn't she like it here? She left all her things behind. What does she expect us to do with it all? There is nothing that we can do with it, except count it, except look carefully through it, and we have done that already.

We back away, us, the house, towards keyholes and gaps. Now there is the house and there are the other things. We have retreated. They have become left-behind things. They have become awkward and extra, things that don't belong. It is inevitable.

★

Now we notice what we didn't notice before: that the paint is actually a strange blue, a cold blue, a blue that wasn't the right decision. We don't want that blue any more. We pick at it and bits fall on to the carpet. We notice how thin the carpet is getting. We notice how the clocks make the walls sound hollow. We don't like the walls to sound hollow so we stop the hands on one or two clocks, but only on one or two, and maybe we loosen the battery in the back of another.

Sometimes a light shines through the window and it looks as if someone has turned on a light downstairs. Sometimes a voice calls through the house, we feel some weight on the stairs; or a coat, a dress left hanging in a cupboard seems rounder, body-shaped, like there is someone inside it. There is a flash on a door handle as if a hand were reaching out to open it, but there is no hand. We are the only ones left.

Things we miss about the one who left suddenly in the night:

> Her laugh, which was as loud and sudden as the gas flame igniting in the boiler.
> The kettle's click and whoosh and teaspoons tapping like rain against the windows.
> Her television with all its bright colours and its other houses.
> The way she jumped when the doorbell rang.

The way we had to make sure the walls caught her when she stumbled.

That smokiness brews up and gets into the curtains. We don't know where it comes from. There is a spider's web behind a door handle and one under a light switch. We like spiders; they are quiet and make good use of the space.

Leaves come in under the door and we pick them up by their stalks and let them out through the letterbox.

Somebody comes and turns off the fridge and the freezer and the boiler. Perhaps we have seen her before. We are not good with faces. For a moment, we think that the woman who left in the night has come back. This new person watches as the freezer shudders, then starts to drop pieces of ice. She stands there, watching. She doesn't do anything except watch as the ice drops and melts on the floor.

Now that there is no noise from the fridge and the freezer and the boiler, we can hear other things. We can hear the pictures beginning to tilt off centre.

The telephone has been left plugged in and sometimes it rings. Sometimes we hear a familiar voice, always saying the same thing: 'I'm not here at the moment. Please leave a message and I'll get back to you.' It is strange, hearing that voice again, and we look around, half expecting to see someone. At least, we think the voice is familiar – we are not good with voices. It is easy for us to forget.

Sometimes we listen to the messages but we do not understand them.

'Hello, I thought I'd ring for a quick catch-up. It's been a long time. Sorry it's been so long. How is everything?'

'The book you ordered is now ready to be picked up.'

'Is this the right number? Do you still live here?'

The shoes are packed into boxes and the boxes are stacked up like bricks. The mirrors are taken down and the walls are just walls again, which is a relief.

There is always somebody who sorts through the left-behind things and turns off the boiler. The woman's footsteps are light and slow. She stares out of the window. She talks on the phone. She puts on one of the jumpers from the wardrobe and wears it all the time, even when she's asleep. It is too small for her. Once, she drops a glass as she is packing, and she looks down at the pieces and then drops the rest, glass by glass, which is probably the clumsiest thing we have ever seen.

She takes the cushions off the sofa and moves it away from the wall. There is something in the empty space. There are small round balls, made out of butter, covered in dust and hair. The woman who left in the night used to cover them in sugar and make anyone who came over eat them. We didn't know that most people dropped them behind the sofa. We didn't know they were there. They are covered in dust and hair. The woman with light, slow footsteps puts her hand over her mouth and stares down at the butterballs. We didn't know they were there. It is not our job to clear things away. They are the only thing we have ever missed.

The house is bare. People come and go, mostly in pairs.

We didn't know those butterballs were there. They are the only thing we have ever missed.

'Would this be our bedroom? I'm not sure if I see this as our bedroom,' they say. They say, 'What do you think?' They look at their reflections in the windows and they look faint and lost. They keep to the edges of the rooms. They sit on the edge of the bath and look down into the plughole. They investigate the pale grey fingerprints on a wall. They lean backwards and measure out invisible objects with their arms.

They are always drawn to the attic. We don't know why.

★

Things left behind in the attic:

    A rocking horse with a missing eye.

    A plastic skull.

    A suitcase stuffed full of receipts and discount vouchers.

    A roll of carpet.

    A cricket bat and a deflated football.

    Four nails and six drawing pins.

    A bunch of dry white flowers.

The attic is a strange place. There are gaps and spaces that lead outside. There are silverfish and seeds and pollen and old cooking smells. Buddleia is growing through the wall. There are things that people have hoarded and left behind.

Once, somebody's legs went through the attic floor because they weren't careful. They didn't step in the right places. Just their legs dangling and us wringing our hands and watching. Plaster everywhere. It is our job to protect the house. Why do they always want to go into the attic? We don't know why.

The buddleia shrivels and dries to husks. The cold enters the house and so does someone new. The boiler is switched on and there are boxes. He moves them in himself, without any help. Most of the boxes are left in the second bedroom and they are not unpacked. There are no proper beds. He unrolls a mat and sleeps on it. He stays up late, staring at the television or at the computer. The room flickers blue and green. He goes to the fridge, to the sofa, to the bathroom, and on his way between rooms he knocks into the walls with his shoulders.

We dream, and in our dream there is a sudden rush of water. Doors and windows soak and split. They lift away from their frames and disappear. Lampshades and clocks float past.

Two children come. The man makes them food and puts it on their plates in the shape of a face. He hadn't turned the oven on before they arrived. The boy looks pleased with his food but the girl scowls and picks at the eyes. The table is too small for three people so they keep knocking knees and elbows. 'What do you want to do?' the man asks them. He isn't eating anything. They shrug. 'Is there a cat here? You said you would get a cat.'

'I haven't got a cat yet,' he says.

'You said you would get one,' they tell him. They look around at the bare house.

We have seen cats before. They stare at us and bristle. We don't like them. We have seen children before. They move around so quickly that we can't keep track of which room they are in. These children are different. They don't move quickly; they kick at the edges of things. They don't seem interested in the house. They trail after each other and when they sit, they fall back with all of their weight so that the sofa bumps into the wall.

★

Now and again, when the children aren't there, a woman comes over to stay. We don't know if we recognise her. We aren't very good with faces. Sometimes, when she goes to the bathroom, she turns up the television first, but we don't know why she would do this. We are probably the only ones who notice. When she can't find her watch, we find it for her, and put it in the pocket of her coat, but then she shouts that she has already looked in the pocket of her coat. We were only trying to help. It is not our job to find things. They step on each other's feet in the kitchen. They move their chairs closer together, slowly, during dinner.

'What are you thinking about?' she asks him, smiling, leaning close.

He looks at his fork. 'The Spanish Revolution,' he says.

'OK,' she says. 'OK.'

They raise their forks and lower them in unison.

Number of tiles on the roof: 874. There were 876 but two disappeared and no one has replaced them.

Leaves come in under the door and we post them out through the letterbox.

Two new ones. They keep close together. There is only ever one light on because they are always in the same room. They don't have any real furniture; they have furniture that doesn't look solid. You can fold it. We have never seen folding furniture. There's no fridge yet, only a gap where the fridge should be. They keep their milk in a saucepan of cold water. We are not sure how well they will look after the house. Nothing they have looks solid.

On their first night, they drink a lot and then dance around the bare room without music. They are lighter than the others – when they walk the boards barely creak. They use more of the space, too, flinging themselves into every corner of the room. They sit first in one place and then another. They are moving all the time. They are touching all the time: if one leaves the room the other one follows soon after. They leave the bathroom door open and their dinner plates unwashed.

The windows are huge and black without curtains.

They have put up a shelf and they have done it badly. It is going to fall off. We know it is going to fall off. We can feel the screws loosening millimetre by millimetre. We can feel the shelf slipping. We knock off a book, then another book, to try to make them notice. They don't notice. The man picks up one of the books and reads out loud from it. 'Listen to this,' he says. We listen. The woman listens.

We don't like them very much. They look after each other more than they look after the house.

There is a night when, as if from nowhere, bright lights and flashes fill the house. We can smell smoke. Whenever this happens we think that perhaps it is the end of the house, but it is never the end of the house. They watch the flashes, their noses pressed up to the glass. They write their names in their own breath and their names stay embedded in it. We can see all the names that have been drawn on the windows, looped and layered over each other. We don't watch the flashes. We prefer to hide from them with our hands over our ears, waiting for them to stop.

They get a piano and put it in the empty room. He plays and she stands behind him with her eyes closed. The music spreads through the house like hot-water pipes. We have never heard noises like it.

They shower together before leaving in the mornings, slipping their bodies around each other in the water. It is like only one person lives here. Their dips in the sofa are just one big dip in the middle. They live with only one light on, in the one room they are both in. We straighten their shower curtain to stop it getting mouldy. We shouldn't have to do such things.

★

The shelf falls. It makes us jump, even though we knew it would happen.

'How's the book?' he calls through from the kitchen where he is doing the washing-up.

She is reading, her feet curled up under her. 'Hmm? I already got milk,' she says, turning a page. 'I already got milk.'

He fumbles with a wet plate and water sloshes down his knees.

The shower switches on. It switches off. The man gets out, and after a pause, the woman gets in. The shower switches on and off again. This is much better. It allows the humid air to cool and disappear. This is much better. Maybe finally they are learning to look after the house.

They tread carefully and slowly – there is no jumping or dancing. They buy solid furniture. The lights are switched off earlier than usual and the television is on almost all of the time. They don't come back as early as they used to – they come home separately and later, sometimes covered in tinsel and glitter. They bring a tree into the house and we notice every needle that drops.

Other people come and they fold out a spare bed. They all sit together and look at the house. They have never paid this much attention. One of the new people is a curtain-straightener, a cushion-plumper. She insists on doing the dishes then purses her lips every time someone carries in another plate. When a bird crashes into the window she doesn't jump. She refolds the towels. 'The shelves you put up aren't straight,' she tells the man. She straightens out the shower curtain so it doesn't go mouldy. We like her very much and are sad when she leaves.

We have seen this before. All day, the woman has been pacing between the bathroom and the bedroom. Her steps are slow and heavy. She flushes the toilet and the pipes sing and hiss. Then she walks back into the bedroom, stands still in the doorway and then lowers herself on to the edge of the bed. Then she gets up again and paces. Then she lies down quietly on the bed. She is already carrying herself differently. We have seen this before.

The man starts coming downstairs in the night. He opens the fridge door and watches the light spill out on to his bare feet. Sometimes, he pulls open the front door and stands on the mat. The cold air rushes into the house. We shiver and get impatient. Why doesn't he close the door? He stands like that for a long time, until something makes him sigh and shut the door and go back upstairs.

★

The piano has disappeared. They have replaced it with a small bed and other noises and mess and lights clicking on and off, endlessly.

The boy is in the attic again. He is always in the attic now that he can walk up the stairs by himself. He is a small boy and he doesn't weigh very much. We know this because he fits easily through the hatch and he doesn't make the floor creak as if his legs will go through the ceiling. We don't have to worry about him going through the ceiling. He likes to be in empty rooms. He likes gaps and small spaces. Once, he hid (we knew where he was) and nobody could find him. A lot of people came to look. We knew where he was all along – inside the rolled-up carpet, for hours.

He has a tiny bird in a box. Three times a day he comes into the attic and leans over it. He puts little things in there. When he leaves, he pulls the suitcase in front of the box. 'Marty, Marty, Marty,' he sings to it. 'Marty, Marty, Marty.' This is what we have learnt from children bringing animals inside the house in boxes: never name them, never ever name them.

He stares at the box for a long time. Then he closes the lid and takes it away.

★

Conversations the boy has with himself, or with someone we can't see:

> Do birds sleep while they are flying?
>
> I am a ghost and no one can see me unless I want them to.
>
> If everybody else disappeared, would it be boring?

He also sings, whistles, hisses, burps and clicks. He is like a miniature house.

Warm light comes through the windows and lies in slabs on the floor.

The buddleia is growing back. The woman comes up to the attic and tells the boy to go downstairs. She hasn't been in the attic for a long time. When the boy has gone, she does the strangest thing. She gets on to the rocking horse and she doesn't fall through the ceiling.

Brick by brick by brick, more houses are being built somewhere near by. When do we arrive in them? We don't know. Were we already there and the house was built around us? We don't know. We don't exist without bricks and slate and glass, and bricks and slate and glass do not exist without us. There is no need to think about it any further, but sometimes we like to think about it a little bit.

The boy makes louder noises and puts more weight on the floorboards and stairs: bang bang

bang. He doesn't go up to the attic now. He stays in his bedroom with the door and the curtains closed.

One day he disappears, but nobody seems worried this time. We can't find him anywhere in the house. No one else is looking. The house goes back to the way it was. There is only a toothbrush left behind in the pot, the banister he pulled off hanging askew. The house gets its quietness back; it gets its echoes and its quietness. Once or twice, the man goes into the boy's bedroom, talking, as if he has forgotten that the boy isn't there.

Things we miss about the boy who left:

> The girl who came to visit him and wrote her name behind a corner of the wallpaper and then stuck it back down with spit. The smell of the stuff he put on his hair – sometimes we would take off the lid and scoop out tiny little bits.

The house is bare. People come and go, mostly in pairs.

When they come in the front door, they bring with them one or two dry leaves, one or two variations of light, and then the door closes and the light is the same.

★

There are dark patches on the walls in the shape of furniture and pictures that aren't there any more. The rocking horse nods forwards. The carpet is thin and threadbare. Why doesn't anyone replace it? We would have replaced it by now. Light moves up the stairs and then down the stairs, and the house is dark again.

We miss lamps. We didn't think we would. We must have got used to them. At night, colours ebb away as if they were never there. The corners of the house darken and the hallway becomes narrower. A door bangs open and closed but we don't know which door it is. It isn't one of our doors. We would never bang our doors like that. It makes us nervous. We miss lamps. The windows are huge and dark. The curtains are still here, they usually take away the curtains. One night, we decide to close them. It is not our job to close them but we prefer it when they are closed.

At night, the house closes into itself and then it stills and quietens and sleeps, and we dream of it under water.

A strong breeze comes in under the door and chases us around the house. It slams a loose cupboard door. It furls and unfurls the corner of a loose piece of wallpaper in a bedroom. Underneath, someone had written something, which they shouldn't have done because that will be hard to get off and we can't remember who it was.

It's always the same – feet, feet, feet and dirt on the carpet and now everything is being moved, now everything is being changed. There is noise and there is more noise and then there is the worst thing: walls have been taken away and a door. Now there is a gap where the door was and there is a bigger room instead of two rooms and one less room where the wall was before. We have been rearranged. We hide behind the curtain poles and under the loose tiles in the kitchen. Things have been changed and things have been taken away. We are not sure. We are not sure at all. We have been rearranged. It is not what we expected to happen. How can you take away a wall or a door and not expect the whole house to fall down? How hasn't the whole house fallen down already? We cower, covering our heads, waiting for it to happen.

It hasn't happened yet.

The man who did all the moving and all the rearranging is staying here with a woman. They have put in a new carpet. We actually liked the old carpet. We actually miss the old carpet. They don't get up early and leave for most of the day like most of the others. Instead, they stay in bed for most of the morning and they eat breakfast in bed and get crumbs everywhere. We are not sure about them. But the woman sings in the shower and her voice is deep and beautiful, almost like the piano, and the man downstairs in the kitchen starts humming the same tune and it seems like he hasn't noticed he is doing it. They stand under the crack in the bathroom ceiling. They say it looks like an ear; they say it looks like a heart. Why are they so good at finding bits of themselves drawn on to the house?

We miss the piano.

They talk about things they are going to do to the house. They are going to get rid of the crack in the bathroom. They are going to pull out the buddleia. They are going to paint everything. They are going to rearrange more walls. We don't want to listen, but we have to listen. It seems like they have nothing to do except change the house. We push against the wall when they're drilling and break their drills. We cling to the wallpaper. It is our job to protect the house.

Now they have gone away and they have covered everything with sheets. We like everything covered with sheets. It keeps everything clean and less dusty. It is not our job to dust.

Sometimes we think of the butterballs. They are the only thing we have ever missed.

The new carpet is fraying. There is no stopping it. The buddleia is growing back. There is no stopping that, either.

Shadows that have passed across the keyhole:
>   twelve.

Number of silverfish in the attic:
>   seven, but one is not moving.

Dust that has floated past so far:
>   four million, seven hundred and forty-eight
>   pieces. There is a lot less dust than you'd think
>   when a house is empty.

Number of times we have banged into a wall,
forgetting that things have been changed:
>   too many to count.

We dream, and in our dreams, there are whole
houses under water, and streets and trees. It is cold
and quiet. Bubbles rise slowly out of chimneys.

They have come back. We think they are the same
people but we are not sure. We are not good with
faces. They seem much older. They walk slowly up
the stairs. They only take some of the sheets off the
furniture. The woman stays in bed, not just late
into the morning but for the whole day. The man
lowers her gently into water. He sponges her back
and washes her hair, keeping her propped upright.
He is silent, he is concentrating hard. We, the
house, hold our breath.

And we must have lost track of time because when
we release it, the house is bare again. The rocking
horse nods forwards. The air slows and stills in

rooms. Nothing is ever exactly the same, but it goes back to how it was. We watch the door and wait for somebody to come through it.

The Authors

Lisa Blower went to Sheffield Hallam University (BA Hons) and the University of Manchester (MA Novel Writing). She worked for over a decade in commercial radio – Kiss, Galaxy, Kerrang – in marketing and events before returning full time to academia and becoming a writer in 2006.

Lisa has a PhD in Creative and Critical Writing from the University of Bangor, where she taught Creative Writing until the birth of her daughter in 2012. Her story 'Broken Crockery' won The Guardian's National Short Story Competition in 2009 and she has spent the past 12 months writing during her daughter's naps. 'Barmouth' was predominately composed after the 4am feed. She has just completed her debut novel *Sitting Ducks*. Lisa grew up in Stoke on Trent – a place which continues to inspire her writing – and now lives in Shropshire.

Lavinia Greenlaw is a poet and novelist and Professor of Poetry at the University of East Anglia. Her collections include *Minsk* (2004) and *The Casual Perfect* (2011). Her first novel, *Mary*

George of Allnorthover (2001) won France's Prix du Premier Roman Etranger. Her second, *An Irresponsible Age* (2006) was followed by two books of non-fiction: *The Importance of Music to Girls* (2007) and *Questions of Travel: William Morris in Iceland* (2011). Her next book of poetry, *A Double Sorrow: Troilus and Criseyde*, will be published in February 2014.

In 2000, Lavinia was given a three-year NESTA fellowship in order to pursue her interest in landscape and perception. In 2011, she received the Ted Hughes Award for her sound installation Audio Obscura. She was the first artist-in-residence at the Science Museum and also held a residency at The Royal Society of Medicine. She is a Fellow of the Royal Society of Literature. Her work for BBC radio includes programmes about the experience of light in Arctic midsummer and midwinter, the darkest place in England, the solstices and equinoxes, Emily Dickinson and Elizabeth Bishop. She also writes radio drama and opera libretti, most recently a version of *Peter Pan* with the composer Richard Ayres, which will be performed at the Welsh National Opera and Covent Garden. Lavinia was born and lives in London.

Sarah Hall is the author of *Haweswater (2003)*, which won the Commonwealth Writers Prize for Best First Novel, a Society of Authors Betty Trask

Award, and a Lakeland Book of the Year prize. Her second novel, *The Electric Michelangelo* (2004), was shortlisted for the Man Booker Prize, the Commonwealth Writers Prize (Eurasia region), and the Prix Femina Étranger, and was longlisted for the Orange Prize for Fiction. Her third novel, *The Carhullan Army* (2007) won the John Llewellyn Rhys Prize, the James Tiptree Jr. Award, a Lakeland Book of the Year prize, was shortlisted for the Arthur C. Clarke Award for science fiction, and long-listed for the Dublin IMPAC Award. Her fourth novel, *How To Paint A Dead Man* (2009) was longlisted for the Man Booker prize and won the Portico Prize for Fiction. Her first collection of short stories, *The Beautiful Indifference* (2011) won the Portico Prize for Fiction and the Edge Hill Short Story prize. It was also short-listed for the Frank O'Connor Prize.

She has taught at a number of creative writing institutions, such as Arvon, Faber Academy and *The Guardian*. She has written plays for the BBC, presented radio and television programmes, and reviewed for the *Guardian*, the BBC, and the *Independent*. She has also judged prestigious literary awards such as The John Llewellyn Rhys Prize, the David Cohen Prize for Literature and the Northern Writers Awards. She was chosen as one of the Granta Best Young British Novelists in 2013. Sarah was born in Cumbria and now lives in Norwich.

Lionel Shriver is the author of 11 novels. She is well-known for the *New York Times* bestsellers *So Much for That* (2010) – a finalist for the National Book Award and the Wellcome Trust Book Prize – and *The Post-Birthday World* (2007) – *Entertainment Weekly's* Book of the Year and one of *Time's* top ten for 2007. Her international bestseller *We Need to Talk About Kevin* (2005) won the Orange Prize, passed the million-copies-sold mark several years ago and was adapted for an award-winning feature film by Lynne Ramsay in 2011. Both this book and *So Much for That* have been dramatised for BBC Radio 4. Her most recent published novel is *Big Brother* (2013). Shriver's work has been translated into 28 languages.

Currently a columnist for *Standpoint*, she is a widely published journalist who writes for the *Guardian*, *The New York Times*, *The Sunday Times*, the *Financial Times*, and the *Wall Street Journal*, among many other publications. Lionel was born in North Carolina in the US and now lives in London.

Lucy Wood completed her BA in English and MA in Creative Writing at Exeter University. Her first book, *Diving Belles* (2012), is a collection of short stories based on Cornish folklore. She has been longlisted for the Frank O'Connor Award and the Dylan Thomas Prize, shortlisted for the Edge Hill Prize and has received a Somerset Maugham Award. Her story, 'Of Mothers and

Little People' was published in the *Telegraph*. She has also had stories broadcast on BBC Radio 4 Extra and as one of the Guardian Short Story Podcasts 2013. She is currently working on her first novel, which is called *Weathering*. Lucy was born in Cornwall and now lives in Exeter.

ALSO AVAILABLE IN THE SERIES:

The BBC National Short Story Award 2010

Featuring:
DAVID CONSTANTINE (WINNER)
JON MCGREGOR (RUNNER UP)
AMINATTA FORNA
SARAH HALL
HELEN OYEYEMI

Foreword by James Naughtie

ISBN 978-1905583348. £6.99
Available on Kindle, Kobo and Apple Store.

The BBC National Short Story Award is one of the world's largest awards for a single short story. All five shortlisted stories, including the winner, are published here side by side. The Award is designed to honour Britain's finest short story writers and to re-establish the importance of the short story as a central literary form.

This year's shortlist brings together a high calibre group of new and established authors exploring human relationships at their most dysfunctional and yet sustaining. Splintered families, the persistence of love, the public versus the private, and the plight of the outsider all provide a recurring focus for the authors in the running for the prize, which marks its fifth year in 2010. The panel of judges this year includes the author and *Guardian* journalist Kamila Shamsie, author and poet Owen Sheers, author Shena MacKay, BBC Editor of Readings, Di Speirs and the *Today* programme's James Naughtie, who also introduces the collection.

ALSO AVAILABLE IN THE SERIES:

The BBC National Short Story Award 2011

Featuring:
D.W. WILSON (WINNER)
JON MCGREGOR (RUNNER UP)
M.J. HYLAND
ALISON MACLEOD
K. J. ORR

Foreword by Sue MacGregor

ISBN 978-1905583416. £6.99
Available on Kindle, Kobo and Apple Store.

'We are living through a golden moment in the history of the short story,' wrote *The Guardian* recently, and the annual BBC National Short Story Award is both a testament to this, and one of the reasons why we are. Now in its sixth year, the Award supports and showcases Britain's best new short fiction and continues to champion the short story as a central literary form.

Themes of desire, envy and disconnection provide recurring motifs for the five shortlisted stories presented here – the extremes that love can endure and what happens when love is not enough. The panel of judges this year included novelist Tessa Hadley, novelist and critic Geoff Dyer, poet and author of *Submarine*, Joe Dunthorne and BBC Editor of Readings, Di Speirs. The panel was chaired by broadcaster Sue MacGregor who also introduces the selection.

The BBC International Short Story Award 2012

Featuring:
MIROSLAV PENKOV (WINNER)
HENRIETTA ROSE-INNES (RUNNER UP)
LUCY CALDWELL   JULIAN GOUGH
M.J. HYLAND   KRYS LEE
DEBORAH LEVY   CHRIS WOMERSLEY
ADAM ROSS   CARRIE TIFFANY

Foreword by Clive Anderson

ISBN 978-1905583515. £8.99
Available on Kindle, Kobo and Apple Store.

"I'm sorry I wrote you such a long letter," quipped Blaise Pascal famously, "I didn't have time to write you a short one."

Brevity may be the soul of wit, but as Clive Anderson argues in his introduction to this collection, it is also, very often, the hard-won soul of great literature. What remains unsaid – just as much as what is said – distinguishes a great story: whether it is through subtle gaps in a narrative or the intentional concealment of things.

In 2012, to mark the London Olympics, the BBC has opened the Award up to English-speaking writers from around the world. The ten shortlisted stories assembled here – from as far afield as South Africa, North America, Australia, Ireland and the Balkans – show the extraordinary diversity and richness of the short story as a truly global form. This year's judges included authors Anjali Joseph, Ross Raisin and Michèle Roberts, BBC Editor of Readings, Di Speirs, and the broadcaster and comedian Clive Anderson, who also chaired the panel.

About The BBC National Short Story Award

The BBC National Short Story Award is one of the most prestigious for a single short story and celebrates the best in home-grown short fiction. It is managed by the BBC in partnership with Booktrust and is now in its eighth year. The Award's ambition is to expand opportunities for British writers, readers and publishers of the short story.

The winning author receives £15,000, the runner-up £3,000 and the three further shortlisted authors £500 each. All five shortlisted stories are broadcast on BBC Radio 4's *Front Row* programme.

The previous winners are: Miroslav Penkov (in 2012, when the Award accepted international entries to commemorate the Olympics); D. W. Wilson (2011); David Constantine (2010); Kate Clanchy (2009); Clare Wigfall (2008); Julian Gough (2007) and James Lasdun (2006).

Award Partners

BBC Radio 4 is the world's biggest single commissioner of short stories. Short stories are broadcast every week attracting more than a million listeners. www.bbc.co.uk/radio4

Booktrust is an independent reading and writing charity responsible for a number of successful national reading promotions, sponsored book prizes and creative reading projects aimed at encouraging readers to discover and enjoy books. www.booktrust.org.uk

Keep up to date with the Award at www.booktrust.org.uk/bbcnssa and by following @Booktrust and #BBCNSSA on Twitter.